"You haven't been listening to me, Sher. I said you're mine now."

"David, I—"

"Shhh," he said. "I'm kissing you."

"You are?" Sheridan whispered.

"I am."

And he was.

David kissed Sheridan so softly, so fleetingly that for a moment she wasn't sure that he had. In the next instant he gathered her tightly into his arms and covered her mouth with his. Desire surged through her, swirled over her senses and sent them into a tumbling, spiraling tangle of passion.

She sank her fingers into his thick hair and he cupped her face in his hands to bring their lips closer and closer together. He embraced the slender column of her throat, and she closed her eyes as the pleasure-giving sensations consumed her.

"Oh, Sher," David said, taking a ragged breath as he lifted his head. "I've never wanted anyone the way I do you. You've cast a spell over me, and I'm powerless to resist you . . ."

WHAT ARE *LOVESWEPT* ROMANCES?

They are stories of true romance and touching emotion. We believe those two very important ingredients are constants in our highly sensual and very believable stories in the *LOVESWEPT* line. Our goal is to give you, the reader, stories of consistently high quality that may sometimes make you laugh, sometimes make you cry, but are always fresh and creative and contain many delightful surprises within their pages.

Most romance fans read an enormous number of books. Those they truly love, they keep. Others may be traded with friends and soon forgotten. We hope that each *LOVESWEPT* romance will be a treasure—a "keeper." We will always try to publish

LOVE STORIES YOU'LL NEVER FORGET
BY AUTHORS YOU'LL ALWAYS REMEMBER

The Editors

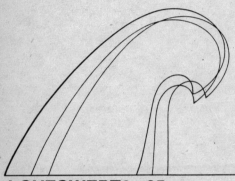

LOVESWEPT® • 85

Joan Elliott Pickart
All the Tomorrows

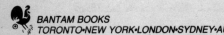
BANTAM BOOKS
TORONTO•NEW YORK•LONDON•SYDNEY•AUCKLAND

ALL THE TOMORROWS
A Bantam Book / March 1985

ISBN 0-553-21700-3

Published simultaneously in the United States and Canada

Bantam Books are published by Bantam Books, Inc. Its trademark, consisting of the words "Bantam Books" and the portrayal of a rooster, is Registered in U.S. Patent and Trademark Office and in other countries. Marca Registrada. Bantam Books, Inc., 666 Fifth Avenue, New York, New York 10103.

PRINTED IN THE UNITED STATES OF AMERICA

O   0 9 8 7 6 5 4 3 2 1

For Candy, who has been there through it all

One

"Take a deep breath, deary, so I can zip this up. There! You're all set."

"Oh, my!" Sheridan gasped. "This is awfully tight, and isn't there something . . . missing? It's rather skimpy."

"Nope, that's it, deary. You'd better get moving. You're due on the trapeze swing in a few minutes."

"Yes, all right," Sheridan said, leaning closer to the mirror for a better look at herself. Goodness, it was obscene, she thought. Her breasts were bulging—bulging, for heaven's sake—over the top of the bright pink satin costume that was also cut high on the sides, revealing a healthy view of her shapely thighs. Gross! The stiff white ruffles standing in rows across her derriere reminded her of a fancy pair of baby's panties. Ridiculous!

A bubble of laughter escaped from Sheridan's lips, and her large blue eyes danced with merriment. The whole thing was so incredibly absurd, she couldn't help but find the humor in the situation. Here she was, Dr. Sheridan Todd, psychologist, specializing in the field of handicapped children at one of the most highly respected private schools in the country, about to swing her little heart out on a trapeze over the crowd in a Las Vegas casino! It was absolutely, totally off the wall!

"Well, here goes nothing!" she said, patting the thick coil of dark hair on her head to be sure it was securely in place.

Sheridan straightened her back, drew herself up to her full height of five feet four, and marched from the dressing room. Actually she shuffled out, curling her toes to keep on the pink satin slippers that were just a bit too large. She made a mental note to wring Janet's neck for getting her into this mess. Janet, that rat, had played on Sheridan's sympathies—and had gotten her half blitzed with three glasses of wine on an empty stomach—so it had all suddenly seemed like a reasonable request.

How tough could it be? Janet had pleaded. Simply sit on a nice little swing for four hours and allow Janet to go camping with her boyfriend. That was crazy enough in itself, Sheridan told herself. People escaped *to* Las Vegas, not *from* it, and Janet knew nothing about roughing it in the wilds. But the current love of her life was the outdoorsy type and, "Please, Sheridan, please fill in for me at the Big Top," Janet had pleaded. "Here, have some more wine," and Sheridan had finally bobbed her head up and down with a crooked grin on her face, saying, "What the heck, why not?"

The noise in the casino was deafening as the slot machines rolled their funny little pictures in front of the magic windows and people laughed and talked with volumes set on high. Cocktail waitresses scurried by, offering drinks courtesy of the Big Top, and an undercurrent of voices saying "Place your bets, please" droned on constantly from the area that held the green felt-covered tables. Everyone appeared to be having a marvelous time and, Sheridan hoped fervently, wouldn't notice the nutty creature zooming overhead.

"Go to that ladder, deary," the woman from the dressing room said. "Barney will follow you up and get you started."

"Wonderful . . . deary," Sheridan mumbled, scooting across the floor to the ladder in question. Goodness, Janet had big feet, Sheridan thought. How in the world was she ever going to keep the slippers on?

"Barney?"

"Yeah? Oh! You're not Janet!"

"I'm filling in for her tonight. What's the plan here?"

"Climb up, get on the swing, and I'll start the mechanical gizmo that will keep it going. Then all you do is sit."

"And remember to hang on."

"I'd recommend it. Ready?"

"No."

"Huh?"

"Yes." Sheridan sighed. "I suppose I am."

She managed to wrap her toes around each rung of the ladder to keep the slippers in place as she tentatively made her way upward. She was acutely aware that Barney was close behind, humming a nondescript tune, and getting a real eyeful of her ruffled bottom. A platform had been constructed approximately thirty feet from the floor, and Sheridan stepped onto it, peering down at the milling throng below.

"Plant your cute little tush on the swing," Barney said in a rather bored voice.

Doing as she was instructed, Sheridan settled herself on the padded seat and tightly gripped the ropes, taking as deep a breath as the constricting costume allowed.

"Okay, doll," Barney said. "Have a nice ride."

"Oh, Lord!" Sheridan shrieked as she was whooshed out across the airy expanse. She shut her eyes as a wave of dizziness swept over her, only to pop them open again as it worsened the sensation of light-headedness. She was a dead person! Her existence was about to come to a screeching halt at the age of twenty-seven and she was too young to die! She wanted to get off this thing! She wanted to go home! She wanted to go to the bathroom!

For the next five minutes Sheridan held on for dear life, every muscle in her body tensing as she went back and forth, back and forth. Slowly she began to relax as the steady rhythm of the swing had a slightly soothing effect on her taut nerves. The fact that the apparatus creaked ominously didn't do much for her peace of mind, but the thing seemed sturdy enough.

All she had to do, Sheridan decided, was pretend she was someplace else. She'd plan her grocery list; mentally write the great American novel; think of her dear, loving Dominic. Lord, if Dominic could see her now, he'd never believe it. Or he'd fall on the floor laughing. Erase the word *fall*, Sheridan told herself. Do not even consider the possibility!

"Oh, no!" Sheridan moaned as one of the satin slippers slid off of her heel. She wiggled her toes upward, trying to balance the wayward material as she jammed her other foot against the sole. This would never do. She looked pigeon-toed and knock-kneed at the same time. Not that anyone was paying any attention to her, but it was dreadfully uncomfortable. She worked her toes slowly along the shiny fabric and had just about managed to push it back onto her heel when the slipper suddenly did a swan dive and headed in the direction of the floor.

"Uh-oh," Sheridan said, peering down and

grimacing as the bright pink object landed squarely on a man's shoulder.

He jumped in startled surprise, grabbed his gift from the heavens, and looked up at Sheridan. "Thanks, honey," he called, waving the slipper in the air. "I'll take it home as a souvenir!"

Sheridan smiled and wiggled her fingers at him, remembering at the last minute not to let go of the rope.

"Hey, sweetcakes, what about me?" a portly man yelled.

"What the hell," Sheridan mumbled, flipping her foot in the air and watching the other slipper sail to the ground, thudding in the general vicinity of the man who had requested it.

"You taking off anything else, hot stuff?" someone hollered, to which Sheridan answered with a vigorous shake of her head.

The excitement apparently over, the spectators returned to what they had been doing, and Sheridan swung on her merry way, deciding she had never been so bored in her entire life. And she really did have to go to the bathroom. Oh, well, she wasn't exactly in a position to raise her hand and ask permission to leave the room!

For the next fifteen minutes Sheridan amused herself by examining the human race from the top down. Strange. There certainly were a lot of men with thinning hair. Poor babies. And the women! Blond hair with dark roots, fat tummies, and drooping back porches. On the other hand there were some nice, wide, manly shoulders. Sheridan was particularly impressed by a pair that were covered in a dark blue sport coat. The crop of hair on the accompanying head was as dark as hers and had a nice sheen to it under the glittering lights. She thought he might be tall, but it was hard to tell. Everyone appeared rather blurred from her vantage point. She could not see his face, but his hands were large and tanned as they moved chips back and forth on the blackjack table where he was playing.

For the lack of something better to do, Sheridan let her imagination take over as she selected a profession for the wide-shouldered gambler. Doctor? Lawyer? Mafia hit man? It would sure help if she could see his face, Sheridan thought. Well, she'd invent one. Rugged high cheekbones, dark eyebrows to match the hair, straight nose, toothpaste-commercial teeth. In short he was beautiful, gorgeous—every woman's dream. Eyes. She'd forgotten eyes. Fathomless pools of a color so dark, you could hardly see the pupils, Sheridan thought dramatically. Eyes that would melt you right down to your socks. Ta-da! He was finished. Perfect from head to toe once she threw in narrow hips, muscular thighs, and a rock-hard chest with curly black hair. Yummy guy. So much for him. She was bored again.

Suddenly Sheridan heard a noise different from the creaking she had become accustomed to. She glanced anxiously around the swing and her eyes widened in horror when she saw that the bolt holding the rope onto the seat on one side was working itself loose! She stared at it, frozen in fear for several long moments as it pulled farther and farther out of its casing. A piercing scream erupted from her throat, and she threw both hands onto the rope on the other side just as the seat gave way, leaving her dangling above the crowded floor.

"My God," someone shouted, "look up there! That girl is in trouble!"

"Help me!" Sheridan yelled. "Please! Someone help me!"

"Get a ladder," a man said.

"That one is attached," Barney said, running

into the throng. "I'll have to go down to the basement."

"Hurry, man, she can't hang on all night!"

Sheridan could hear the buzz of voices, the orders being shouted, and told herself they were coming for her. They had to be! Her arms were already beginning to ache, and her hands felt as if they were on fire from clutching the rough rope. She couldn't look down! The distance to the floor would have multiplied tenfold. God, she was so frightened. A roaring noise started in her ears and black spots danced before her eyes. She was going to faint! Sweet heaven, no!

Suddenly through the chaos a deep, rich voice reached her jumbled mind. It was soothing, stroking her like soft velvet. "Hang on, honey," the Voice said. "Don't panic. Just listen to me, okay?"

"Yes," Sheridan whispered.

"I'm standing on a stool that's on top of the table with an army of guys behind me. I'm directly beneath you. When I say to let go, drop straight down, and I'll catch you. The others will break our fall when we go over."

"No! Oh, no!" Sheridan said, a sob catching in her throat.

"Hey, you're not going to cheat me out of my chance to be a hero, are you?" the Voice said, the gentle resonance causing Sheridan to take a steadying breath.

"I—I guess not," she said.

"That's my girl. Okay, I'll count to three and you open your hands. Trust me, babe. We're going to be a terrific team."

At that moment Sheridan would have believed the Voice if he had told her he was going to flap his wings and fly up and get her. She was nearly hypnotized by a combination of fright and the rich timbre of the Voice.

"One . . . two . . . three!"

Sheridan let go!

An instant later strong arms grabbed her roughly around the waist and pulled her back against a brick-wall body. The impact sent them toppling backward as a shout went up from a multitude of voices, and with a resounding thud they landed in a tangled mass of humanity. Sheridan had squeezed her eyes tightly closed before releasing her hold on the rope and now opened them tentatively. Somehow she had gotten turned around and was lying facedown on top of the Voice, who still held her tightly in his arms. She was staring into dark eyes that were surrounded by the rugged, tanned, handsome face she had invented for the wide-shouldered man in the blue sport coat!

"Hello," the Voice said, smiling and producing the toothpaste-commercial teeth. "Fancy meeting you here."

" 'lo," she mumbled.

"Hey," someone yelled, "undo this jigsaw puzzle. There's a jerk sitting on my head!"

The Voice chuckled, causing Sheridan to bounce up and down on his chest. "No hurry," he said softly, "my view is terrific."

Sheridan gasped as she realized the man's dark gaze was roaming leisurely over her full breasts that still bulged above her costume and were being crushed against his chest.

"Would you please let me up?" she said, her cheeks flushed and warm.

"Can't. There's guys pinning my arms. Aren't I comfortable to lie on? I personally think this is rather nice."

It was just too much! It really was! Sheridan suddenly burst into laughter, lowering her head and burying it in the man's shoulder.

"Is this funny?" he asked. "Or are you hysterical?"

"I can't believe it," she said merrily, lifting her head again. "It's bizarre! Unreal! Oh! Thank you for saving my life."

"That's it? Just thank you?"

"Thank you very much?"

"Who's on my foot?" a man bellowed. "What's the hold up? Get me out of here!"

"Don't laugh," Sheridan said to the Voice. "It . . . jiggles me."

He laughed.

She blushed again.

"Back to the debt you owe me," he said.

For someone who claimed he had been rendered immobile, he was fast on the draw, Sheridan thought. Strong fingers slid around the nape of her neck, and lips that were soft and sensuous pressed against hers in a kiss that sent tingles spiraling through her body. It went on and on, and Sheridan again heard the rushing noise in her ears.

"That," the man said, when he finally released her, "was a lovely down payment."

"Okay, Superman," someone said, "you're clear. Let's get this little girl on her feet and see if she's all right."

The Voice lifted Sheridan up and planted her firmly on her bottom on the green felt table, then swung his long legs over the edge and dropped to the floor. He turned immediately to face her, a frown on his handsome face. It was really him! The man she had conjured up in her imagination while she had been swinging. The same straight nose, dark eyebrows, the fathomless deep pools of his eyes, the—

"I think we ought to have a doctor check you over," he said.

"No, I'm fine," Sheridan said.

"The casino will pay for it."

"Here's your coat, buddy," a man said, handing over the blue sport jacket that Sheridan wasn't the least surprised to see. "She ought to sue this place."

"Want to sue?" the Voice asked, shrugging into his jacket.

"No." Sheridan laughed. "I'd really like to get out of here though."

"Your wish is my command." He smiled and scooped her off the table, then set her on her feet.

"Oh, ow! Oh!" Sheridan yelled.

"What's wrong?"

"My ankle."

Again she was lifted into strong arms and held next to the hard chest. "Say good-bye and thank you to all our helpful friends," the man said.

"What? Oh, thank you, everyone. You were wonderful!" Sheridan said.

A chorus of farewells followed them as the man carried her across the floor of the casino. Then the players immediately resumed their earlier activities.

"Wait a minute!" Sheridan said. "Where are you taking me?"

"To have your foot looked at. We'll find an emergency room at some hospital and—"

"No! I'm not going anywhere dressed like this!"

"Where are your clothes?"

"In that dressing room over there. I'll hop in on one foot and—"

"Heavens, no! You don't know how badly you're injured. You can't go bouncing around."

"But—"

"Man in the room!" he hollered as he strode into the dressing area. Sheridan rolled her eyes.

"That you are, darlin'," said a buxom blonde, who was wearing only a towel. "And a nice package of meat on the hoof! You stayin' long?"

"Nope," the man said. "Just dropped by for a minute to pick up a few things."

"There," Sheridan said, pointing to a dressing table.

"Comin' back later, sugar?" the blonde said.

"Doubt it." The man leaned over so Sheridan could shovel her clothes into her arms.

"Well, damn, darlin', I'm just real disappointed in y'all. By the way, my name is Candi. What's yours?"

"David. See ya, Candi."

"Surely do hope so, David honey. Bye."

David, Sheridan thought as he carried her out of the room. It fit. Not Dave. Certainly not a wimpy Davie. Just David. Very good. But why was she allowing this man to tote her around like a sack of potatoes? She didn't even know him! "Halt!" she said.

"Halt?"

"Yes, as in stop! Look, I really appreciate what you've done for me. You could have been seriously injured when I came flying at you like that. But I must insist you put me down. You're a total stranger and—"

"I certainly am not!" he said indignantly. "I saved your life, remember? Plus, we shared a very delicious kiss while that nifty little body of yours was lying on top of mine. Did you notice how well we fit together? And last but definitely not least, you jiggled not two inches away from my nose. I'd say we know each other extremely well."

Sheridan frowned. "You're crazy."

David smiled. "You're cute. This is better than the time a girl jumped out of a cake at a bachelor party I went to. Of course, you've got more clothes on than she did, but there were a dozen guys in that room.

You fell out of the sky right into my arms and you're all mine."

"I beg your pardon?"

"What's your name?"

"Name?"

"You know, the thing people call you when they want to get your attention?"

"Yes, my name. Uh, Sherry."

"Ah, like the sweet, mysterious drink. Perfect."

"David, put me down this instant! I want to get dressed and—"

"Shall I carry you into the ladies' room?"

"No!"

"Oh. Well, there's a chair over there in the corner. You can put your stuff on over the top of your zoot suit. Seems a shame though. I really like that little outfit."

David set Sheridan on the chair, and she hastily pulled on her red flannel shirt and buttoned it over the pink satin costume. She leaned over and peered at her ankle, moaning silently when she saw that it was beginning to swell. Gingerly poking her foot into the leg of her jeans, she repeated the process with the other and voiced no objection when David held her arm as she balanced herself precariously and pulled up the jeans.

"What's wrong here?" Sheridan frowned, tugging on the material. "Lord, it's the ruffles on my rear end. I can't zip my pants!"

"Interesting problem," David said thoughtfully.

"Ducky. Just really ducky!"

"Your shirttail is pretty long, so just take the jeans off. It's the only solution."

"Brother," Sheridan said, sitting back down and removing the pants. "Well, let's try the old loafers on the bummed-up foot."

"Better not. It's swollen and will hurt like hell if you jam it in there."

"David, you can't carry me all over Las Vegas!"

"My Italian mother raised me to assist ladies in distress. Besides, I told you. I caught you, I get to keep you."

"Cute. You sound like a dogcatcher. You're Italian?"

"One hundred percent pure." He grinned.

"That's nice," Sheridan said absently, folding up her jeans. Italian! That accounted for the black eyes, thick dark hair, bronze complexion, and— An Italian Romeo, that's what he was! He was masculinity personified; he oozed sensuality. Lord, listen to her! She sounded as awed as "darlin' Candi." David had the same coloring as her Dominic. Of course, dope, she told herself; they were both Italians!

"Sherry?"

"Who? I mean, what?"

"Ready to go to the hospital?"

"No, I'm not. I'll take a taxi home and put some ice on my foot and—"

"You're not riding around Las Vegas in the back of a cab with no pants on!"

"Oh, dear, I forgot about that. I don't think I can drive my car though."

"Which is why I'm taking you in mine."

"I don't think—"

"You have any choice," he finished for her.

"All right." Sheridan sighed, throwing up her hands. "You win."

"I won you when you landed on me, remember?"

"Would you knock it off? I don't belong to you! Do I look like a Cracker Jack prize?"

David put his head back and roared with laughter; the sound was rich and throaty and made it difficult for Sheridan to keep from smiling. "That," he said, pointing a long finger at her, "was funny! I like you, Sherry Whoever. Do you have a last name?"

"No."

"Oh, I get it. We're adding a bit of mystery to our relationship. Okay, we'll be plain old Sherry and David for now."

"Whatever."

Once again Sheridan was airborne and nestled against David's chest as he backed against the glass doors and walked out into the cool April air. The bright lights of the casinos lining Las Vegas Boulevard seemed to change the night into day. David walked to the rear parking lot of the Big Top and set Sheridan carefully on the hood of the car while he unlocked and opened the door. Then he picked her up again and deposited her on the plush seat. She leaned her head back and sighed wearily, shutting her eyes for a brief moment.

It had been the most incredible night of her life. And now here she was, driving off with a man she didn't know, who— Well, she sort of knew him. But no, not really. It was too late anyway. David had already started the motor and was pulling out of the parking space. She was being kidnapped! Oh, for heaven's sake, how dumb! One thing was very certain. Sheridan was not about to get into a lengthy explanation as to how she happened to be on that idiotic swing in the first place. If she told David she held a doctorate in psychology, he'd never believe her. Just let him deposit flaky little Sherry safely home and be done with it. But then she'd never see him again! How awful! He was so handsome and—

"Which way?" David asked.

"What? Oh, turn left on Las Vegas Boulevard and right on Riviera, then go straight ahead about five miles, and left on Spokane. It's a brick house at the end of the cul-de-sac."

"Got it. Say, have you been swinging around the Big Top long?"

"No, and I won't do it again," Sheridan said adamantly.

"Can't say I blame you, but will you be able to find another job? A lot of people are out of work these days."

"I'll, oh, get by," she said. Lord, she thought, she was digging herself in deeper here. She was such a lousy liar, she'd never keep the facts straight. Might as well just tell him the truth. "Actually, David," she said, "I was filling in for a friend tonight. I'm a psychologist."

"That's rich, Sher," David laughed. "And I'm Sylvester Stallone."

"*I am!*"

"*You're* Sylvester Stallone?"

"No, damm it. I've got a Ph.D. in psychology!"

"Right. Whatever you say." He smiled.

"Oh, just forget it," she said angrily, crossing her arms over her breasts.

"Good idea. It was pretty far-out. You don't have to try and impress me, Sher. I like you just the way you are."

"My name is not Sher, or Sherry either, for that matter. It's Sheridan. Doctor Sheridan Todd."

"Whew. Classy, Sylvester." David chuckled.

"I used to like you, David, but the feeling is fading fast."

"You can't be mad at me! I'm your hero! And you're mine, mine, mine!"

"Are you going to start *that* again?"

He shrugged. "I never stopped."

"David, read my lips. I am not a Kewpie doll you won at a carnival!"

"I know that! You're a trapeze swinger who fell

into my arms and my life, and I intend to keep you. How do you like them apples, kid?"

"Stinko."

"Why? I'm a nice guy. Hey, you're not sewed up with someone else, are you? I'll throw the bum out!" David roared.

"Well," Sheridan said slowly, a picture of Dominic coming to her mind, "I do have a . . . commitment."

"Heavy-duty?"

"For life."

"You're married?"

"No."

"Living together?"

"No."

"Strange arrangement. Can't be that serious," David said. "We'll dust him out of the picture."

"Dominic? Never!" Sheridan said firmly.

"Dominic? My competition is another Italian?"

"One hundred percent pure."

"A worthy opponent then, but I'll win. I can be very charming, Sher."

"It's Sheridan. How old are you, David?"

"Thirty-five. Why? Making comparisons?"

"Of course."

"And Dominic? Is he ancient? With mega-bucks?"

"He's four. I mean, forty!" Sheridan shouted, realizing immediately she had blown it.

"Dominic is a four-year-old kid?" David said, whooping with laughter. "You really had me going there for a minute, Sher."

"Sheridan," she said crossly.

"So you're divorced."

"I've never been married."

"Must be tough raising a boy alone. Man, how are you going to take care of him if you quit your job at the Big Top? Hold it! You don't look Italian."

"I'm English, Welsh, and German."

"Then how did you manage to have a one hundred percent pure Italian baby?" David said, waggling a finger at her.

"He's not exactly mine. Listen, David, it's terribly complicated, I'm exhausted, and that is my house right there. Let's just drop the subject of Dominic, okay?"

"For now."

"David, this little sticker on the dashboard indicates this is a rented car, which tells me you jogged into Vegas for a fun-packed fling and will shuffle off to Buffalo when you're finished."

"No, Los Angeles."

"Mine was a figure of speech meaning your excessive use of the possessive regarding my person is wearing a bit thin because you don't even live here. In other words, clam up!"

"The fact that I presently reside in metropolitan L.A. is an insignificant triviality, sweet Sher," David said, turning off the ignition as he stopped in her driveway. "It will not deter me from satisfactorily completing my mission at hand. You are mine, and will thus so henceforth remain."

"Bull!" she said, opening the door.

"I thought it was a pretty flashy dissertation. Give me your key. I'll unlock your house and come back and carry you in."

"I'll hop, thank you!"

"You move and I'll paddle those ruffles on your tush."

"Damn, you're pushy!"

"Sher, Sher. I'm charming. Remember? I'm dripping with charisma. You're just not paying close enough attention. Now, where's your key?"

"Here!" she said, pulling it out of the pocket of

her jeans and smacking it into the palm of his hand. "And it's Sheridan!"

"Okay, Sher-eye-dan, I'll be right back."

He was driving her nuts! Sheridan thought as David strode across the lawn on his long legs. A few hours ago she was a perfectly sane woman, yet this man had brought her to the edge of a nervous breakdown! Charisma, her big toe! Blatant sexuality, yes. When he kissed her, she thought she would die on the spot. That was potent stuff! But he was crazy! Totally bonkers. He acted as though she were his personal property because he'd kept her from breaking her neck. What a cuckoo. Devastatingly handsome, but weird. Of course, he did have some endearing qualities, but—

"Up you go," David said, leaning into the car. "I may carry you around even after your ankle is better. You sure feel good in my arms."

"Oh, good grief," Sheridan said, circling his neck with her hands and once again aware of the solid wall of David's chest as he pulled her close. The man had a point, she thought as they headed across the lawn. This could become habit-forming.

David had switched on the lights in the living room, casting a soft glow over the area. He placed Sheridan gently on the nubby oatmeal-colored sofa and propped her foot on a throw pillow that he set on the dark wood coffee table.

"Ice. Kitchen," he said.

"That way," she said, pointing him in the proper direction.

"Actually, Sher," David said when he returned a few minutes later with ice cubes wrapped in a towel, "we should have gotten a cold pack on this right away, then moved on to heat. I hope this is going to help."

"Ugh. It's freezing. You sound as though you know what you're talking about. Are you a doctor?"

"Me? No, an ex-jock. I played football at Stanford and spent a lot of time doing the ice-then-heat number."

"Did you consider going pro?"

"I'm not that much into pain." David chuckled. "Say, I really like your place," he said, wandering around the room.

Sheridan watched as David glanced at the stereo, the collection of plants, the full bookcase, and the expensive furniture done in warm earth tones—tan, brown, orange, and yellow. Thick chocolate-brown carpeting covered the floor, and a frown creased David's brow as he looked at several paintings that were hanging on the wall.

"Microwave and dishwasher in the kitchen plus all matching yellow appliances," he said thoughtfully. "I didn't realize being a trapeze swinger paid so well."

"I told you, David, I'm a—"

"Yeah, I know, a psychologist," he said, sitting down next to her. "Are you sure Dominic is only four?"

"Meaning—or is he really my sugar daddy who set me up in this place?" she asked, her blue eyes flashing with anger.

"It doesn't matter to me what you've done in your past, Sher. The future is what's important to us."

"Damn you," she shrieked. "How dare you insinuate that I'm a kept woman! You have a helluva lot of nerve!"

"I'm not passing judgment on your previous lifestyle," he said calmly. "Starting now, however, I'm running the show. No lady of mine is going to accept gifts from—"

"That does it! Get out of my house! Get out! Out! Out! And take your lousy charisma with you!"

"Don't be silly. I'm tending to your injury. How's it doing?"

"It's frozen. Would you leave?"

"Nope," he said, pulling loose his tie. He stuffed it into the pocket of his jacket and undid the two top buttons on his light blue shirt. "Not until I get you into bed."

"What?"

"Don't get so upset. I meant safely tucked in so I'll know you won't go hopping around. I don't intend to make love to a woman with a painful footsie. It would detract from your enjoyment of the event, and when we do make love, it's going to be beautiful for both of us. I'm a patient man. I can wait."

"Aaak!" Sheridan screamed. "I can't take any more of this!"

"The ice is too cold?"

"It's you! You're giving me the crazies!"

"You're just distraught, Sher. You had a very horrifying experience this evening. A good night's sleep and you'll feel a lot better. Trust me."

"Not on your life, bub. I want you to haul it out of here."

"Tomorrow is Sunday. You can stay off that foot and— Oh, I forgot. You don't have a job anymore anyway. That's just as well because you can give that ankle time to heal properly. Are you hungry? Shall I fix you something?"

"No! This is a nightmare. The alarm will go off, I'll wake up, and my life will be back to normal," Sheridan said wearily. "This simply is not happening to me."

"Oh, I'm real all right." David chuckled. "And you and I have just begun. We're going to be great together, Sher. Oh, what kind of car do you have? I'll get it over here to you tomorrow. Is it parked behind the Big Top?"

"David, please." Sheridan moaned.

"Poor Sher." He slipped his arm around her shoulders. "You're all worn out. Wouldn't you be more comfortable without all these pins in your head?" he said, reaching up and pulling them loose.

The thick braided coil tumbled onto her back, and before she could speak, David began to rake his fingers gently through the waist-length hair, spreading it out like a raven fan.

"Beautiful," he said quietly, pushing it aside and kissing the nape of her neck. "You have the most gorgeous hair I have ever seen. I can imagine it spread out over a pillow with moonlight dancing around your lovely face."

"I—" Sheridan started, only to stop as a strange sensation began pulsating in the pit of her stomach and spread through her entire body. Her eyes widened as David tilted her chin up with his finger and slowly lowered his head, claiming her mouth in a sweet, sensuous kiss that left her breathless and trembling.

"Your skin is like velvet," he said, his tone hushed and low as his lips moved to the base of her throat. "Ivory velvet. And your eyes are blue sapphires. Oh, Sher, I'm so glad you fell into my arms. This is the luckiest day of my life. And yours, too, my sweet, because we are going to be sensational together."

"David, don't."

"I won't rush you, Sher," he said, placing nibbling kisses along the slender column of her throat.

"It's Sheridan," she said weakly as desire swept through her like a rampant fire.

"Yes. Yes, I know," he murmured, burying his face in her luscious hair. "Sher-eye-dan."

"Lord!" she said, snapping herself out of her

lethargic trance. "Stop it right this minute! I am sitting here allowing some looney tune named David What's-his-face to whisper sweet nothings in my ear while my foot is turning into a block of ice. I should have myself committed!"

"You're right. That's enough of the cold pack," David said, dropping the towel onto the floor. "And if it will make you feel any better, I'll officially introduce myself."

"Wonderful," Sheridan muttered, gingerly wiggling her toes.

"You see before you in all his splendor the new love of your life, one Mr. David Cavelli," he said with a sweep of his arm.

Sheridan could feel the color draining from her face as her hands flew to her cheeks and her eyes widened in horror. "You're David Cavelli?" she croaked. "Cavelli? Cavelli? Oh, God, tell me you're kidding! You can't be! I— No! You just can't be David Cavelli!"

Two

"Gosh, Sher." David frowned. "Cavelli is a good Italian name. We go back for generations."

"David, I'll be the happiest woman alive if you tell me your parents aren't Rosalie and Edward."

"They are! Do you have ESP?"

"No, I have a headache, a heartache, a death wish," she said, covering her eyes with her hand.

"Hello?" David said, pulling her hand away. "Would you kindly explain how you know who my folks are?"

"David, do you think you could develop amnesia and forget tonight ever happened?"

"Of course not!"

"Didn't think so. Oh, dear heaven, I fall off a swing I had no business being on in the first place, and land on the man who has the power to destroy my career, hopes, dreams, everything."

"Me?"

"You."

"You've lost me, Sher," David said, shaking his head. "I'm not messing up your career. You're the one who said you were quitting the Big Top."

"The jig is up. The whistle has blown," Sheridan said miserably. "David, go into my bedroom."

"Now, Sher, I don't think we should make love until your ankle is—"

"The room! Not the bed! There is a silver frame on the wall with a certificate in it. Go read it, please."

"Okay." He shrugged, then left the room.

Sheridan sat perfectly still, cringing when she heard David yell, "Holy cow!" He immediately strode back into the living room. "It's a diploma," he said, his eyes wide, "saying you're Doctor Sheridan Todd with a degree in psychology!"

"That's me."

"Man," he said, sinking onto the sofa, "my Sher is a genius! When I hold out my arms and catch someone, I do it up right. You understand, Sher, I was going to keep you even when I thought you were a casino swinger. This is just an added bonus."

"You're getting crazy again!"

"Hey, where did you meet my parents?"

"David, listen to me carefully. On Monday you will do the annual visit and report on the Haven School for Handicapped Children, which—"

"You *do* have ESP!"

"Shut up. Which also includes an in-depth update on the staff and their suitability to be associated with the Haven."

"Right, but how—"

"The school is funded by a foundation originally started by your grandfather. Edward Cavelli, your father, usually makes the yearly tour but wasn't feeling up to par so his son David was sent in his place."

"It was in the newspapers!"

"No, David, it was told to us at a faculty meeting. I am the psychologist at the Haven."

"I'll be damned." He grinned. "That's terrific."

"Terrific! Terrific! It's the worst disaster of the year!"

"Why?"

"Think about it! What would your father and grandfather say if they knew a member of the Haven staff had been on that swing tonight?"

"Lord," David said, shaking his head.

"I should never have done it, but I didn't think anyone would recognize me, and my friend Janet was so desperate, and . . . oh, hell. A teacher was fired last year because she wore her skirts too tight and refused to change her wardrobe. Your family's rules and regulations are strict, unreasonable, and probably against the law, but I've never had any problem following the directives. Until now. I'm canned. Booted out. Finished. Kaput."

"Hey, you didn't land on my father. I'm me, *David* Cavelli, remember?"

"I can't ask you to falsify a report. My behavior was inexcusable."

"I just won't tell them, Sher."

"Have you ever lied to your father?"

"Of course not, but—"

"And you can't do it now!"

He smiled confidently. "Sure I can."

"David, we are talking about honor between a father and son!"

"No," he said gruffly. "We are discussing a woman who is obviously dedicated to a profession she loves, who happened to help out a friend. Sher, I am a devoted son, a good Italian boy, but I don't kid myself. I respect my father as a man, but he lives in the Ice Age. Our family has so much money, it's ridiculous, and my mother still asks permission to buy a dress! I am not about to see you lose your job because of a narrow-minded man. No, Sher, I won't tell them."

"David, I—"

"Are you a good psychologist?"

"Damn good."

"And you love those kids at the Haven?"

"Oh, yes! David, that's where my Dominic is!"

"Then it's settled. We're not discussing this any further. You're still mine, but I'll come up with another story about how I met you. Too bad about that. I thought it was great. Plop! There you were."

"Oh, David," Sheridan said, throwing her arms around his neck. "How can I ever thank you?"

He grinned. "Are you really handing me a loaded question like that?"

"No, I guess not, but I am grateful. That's twice in one night you've saved my life."

"True. You're running up quite a bill."

"Excuse me a minute. I'll be right back," Sheridan said.

"No hopping allowed."

"David, I don't know how to make this announcement in a ladylike fashion so I'll just blurt it out. I have to go to the bathroom!"

"Cross my palm with money."

"Ever since I was on the swing!"

"Lots of money."

"David!"

"Yes, ma'am," he said, jumping to his feet. "Right away, ma'am."

David carried her to the appointed room and Sheridan bid him a firm farewell, closing the door on his smiling face. Oh, what bliss to unzip the skin-tight costume and take a deep breath at last, Sheridan thought. She wiggled free of the satin material while leaning against the wall, being very careful not to put any pressure on her throbbing foot. The business at hand completed, she pulled on a floor-length royal-blue velour dressing gown that was hanging on the back of the door and tugged the sash tightly around her tiny waist.

"Oh! You scared me," she said when she opened the door to find David standing directly in front of her.

"Where else would I be? I'm your human taxicab."

"Which must be getting old," she said as he picked her up.

"On the contrary, I'm thoroughly enjoying myself. Where to? Ready for bed?"

"It's not that late and I'm feeling better. I'll sit on the sofa awhile, but this isn't exactly why you came to Las Vegas early. Why don't you go back down on the Strip and gamble?"

"Are you trying to get rid of me?" he said, setting her on the sofa.

"No, but Sin City is beyond those doors, beckoning to you with its glitter and glamor and—whatever."

"I'd rather be with you, Sher."

"Sher." She laughed. "No one has ever called me that."

"Good. A private name for my private lady."

"David, I still feel very bad to think you're going to lie to your father because of me."

"Look at it as an omission of certain unimportant facts. Edward Cavelli, bless his heart, is a loving husband and father; an honest, shrewd businessman; and a prude. Do you know I was still chaperoning my sister on her dates when she was nineteen years old? He was born in the wrong century. I love him, but I sure don't understand him. He would definitely fire you if he knew about your fling on the swing, but he isn't going to find out. Clear?"

"All right, David," Sheridan said softly.

"Now! Tell me about Dominic. He's four. He's Italian. He's at the Haven. What else?"

"Oh, David, he's beautiful," Sheridan said, her eyes shining. "There's a picture of him in there on my dresser. Dominic is bright and funny and I love him so much. I'm trying desperately to adopt him. I want him to be my son, David."

"No wonder you said it was a lifetime commitment. His being at the Haven means he has a handicap. Is it severe?"

"He's partially deaf, but he's reading lips very well, is learning sign language, and is speaking more clearly all the time."

David nodded. "Good for him. Not bad for a little kid. So what's the hang up on your getting him? Is it because you're a single woman?"

"I wish that was all I was fighting. The whole thing is a mass of red tape. Dominic was abandoned in a monastery in northern Italy when he was around two. He was very ill, and the monks nursed him back to health, but later discovered he was losing his hearing. There was an American reporter over there at the time who sent the story back to his editor as a human-interest piece. Your mother heard about Dominic and made arrangements to have him brought to the Haven."

"That sounds like my ma. I guess I was so buried in work, I didn't pick up on it though. Go on."

"Dominic had been at the Haven about a month when I was hired a year and a half ago. He was very withdrawn, wouldn't talk at all, and was totally uncooperative. Oh, David, when I saw him, it was love at first sight. I guess that sounds corny but—"

"No, Sher," David said quietly, "love at first sight is definitely not corny."

"Anyway Dominic and I have become so close. He's a part of my life now and I want him here with me. The problem is, he's not really a citizen of this country, and the Italian courts are blocking the adoption before I even get it started. They feel he may have relatives in Italy who should have him, but no one ever reported him missing. The only identification he had was a scrap of paper that said *Dominic* on it."

"So what do you call him? Dominic Hey You?"

"No, Dominic Cavelli."

"What?"

"It was your mother's idea. She met Dominic when she came for the annual visit with your father last year and decided Dominic should have a last name. That much the courts agreed to. He's legally Dominic Cavelli."

"I'll be damned." David smiled. "I bet my father blew a fuse."

"He did! He was afraid someone would think Dominic was an illegitimate child of one of you virtuous Cavelli boys, but your mother stood her ground."

"Amazing! That's the same lady who asks permission to go to the beauty shop. I assume you have a lawyer working on this?"

"Yes, but he's beginning to feel he's fighting a losing battle trying to plead a case through the mail. He says we need to hire an attorney who is sharp as a tack, speaks Italian, and will go to Italy in person."

"Makes sense."

"Costs big bucks. I've used up my savings on lawyer fees already. If I sell this house, I'll cut my own throat, because Dominic's social worker says having my own home in a good neighborhood like this is a definite plus in my favor. I've got to stay here. Now can you understand why I was so panicked when I thought I'd be fired? I couldn't see my Dominic every day, and it would be on record that I had been let go because of personal misconduct. They'd never allow me to adopt him if that happened."

"It isn't going to."

"Thanks to you."

"I would say, sweet Sher, that you have taken on a mighty big battle."

"I'm going to win, David. Dominic is going to be my son."

"He's a helluva lucky kid. I'm looking forward to meeting him on Monday."

"He's very apprehensive around strangers," Sheridan said.

"I'll be charming." David smiled. "Whip out the ol' charisma."

"Ugh!"

"So, what do you two do together? He's too young for slot machines. The zoo? Picnics?"

"Dominic has some psychological problems," Sheridan said, clutching her hands tightly in her lap. "The social worker suggested I start bringing him home for weekends so it would be in my file that I was sincere in wishing to provide a home for him."

"Smart."

"Six months ago I fixed up the second bedroom for him and—and I was counting the hours until he would sleep in his own bed here. But . . ." She brushed a sudden tear off her cheek.

"Hey," David said, pulling her close to his chest, "take it easy. What happened?"

"Dominic has deep-seated fears from when he was abandoned. Even as his psychologist I didn't know that. The Haven is the only place he feels totally secure. You know that doctors and dentists come to check the children right on the premises."

"Yes."

"Consequently Dominic has never been off the grounds. When I attempted to put him in my car to bring him here, he went hysterical. It was so frightening for both of us. I'm working with him, but it's very slow because he's too young to express verbally what's inside. So not only do I have to convince the

Italian courts to let me have him, I have to show an American judge that Dominic has overcome his insecurities and is ready to live a normal life outside the Haven."

"My God," David whispered. "How can you take on all this alone?"

"I love that child, David."

"What about you, Sher? Don't you want a husband and babies of your own?"

"Yes, I do. But a man would have to accept Dominic as his son and realize there would be certain difficulties because of the hearing problem. I don't expect to find anyone like that. I've made my choice. Dominic and I will be fine together. Just the two of us."

"You are some kind of special lady."

"Not really. I'm a mother who loves her son. That's how I picture my relationship with Dominic. So you see, Mr. Cavelli, you should march yourself back to the Big Top and see if another girl will fall into your lap. You caught the wrong one."

"You haven't been listening to me, Sher. I said you're mine now."

"David, I—"

"Shhh," he said. "I'm kissing you."

"You are?" Sheridan whispered.

"I am."

And he was.

David kissed Sheridan so softly, so fleetingly that for a moment she wasn't sure that he had. In the next instant he gathered her tightly into his arms and covered her mouth with his, parting her lips and thrusting his questing tongue into her sweet mouth. Desire surged through Sheridan, swirled over her senses and sent them into a tumbling, spiraling tangle of passion.

She sank her fingers into his thick hair as he

cupped her face in his hands to bring their flickering tongues closer and closer together. Their breathing became labored as David slid his hands down Sheridan's hair to her waist, then up to caress her full breasts. They responded to his maddening touch even through her velour dressing gown. His lips moved to the slender column of her throat, and she closed her eyes as the pleasure-giving sensations consumed her.

"Oh, Sher," David said, taking a ragged breath as he lifted his head, "I have never wanted anyone the way I do you. You've cast a spell over me, Sher."

"David, you make me feel so— But this isn't going to happen between us. I should never have let you kiss me like that."

"Why not? It was special for both of us."

"You're here for a short time, David, and my life is terribly complicated because of Dominic. You and I, together, spells heartache and I couldn't handle it."

"I'm not going to hurt you, Sher. I found you and I'm not letting go."

"Oh, you Italians! Stubborn as mules!"

"Me and Dominic? Hey, we're top-notch guys."

Sheridan smiled. "And charming?"

"Twenty-four hours a day."

"I think I'll go to bed now. Alone. I'm suddenly very tired."

"It has not been your run-of-the-mill type night. Okay, I'll tuck you in. Man, I am going to use up my life's supply of willpower when I put you in that bed and walk away. Oh, I'll get your car over here tomorrow. Don't argue. I have your keys in my pocket. Is it at the Big Top?"

"Yes, but—"

"Taxi time," he said, and swung her up into his arms.

David set Sheridan on the foot of the double bed

and pulled back the blankets. He then placed her carefully on the cool sheets and tugged the covers into place. Sheridan's hair spread out in a shining raven swirl, and David quickly straightened.

"I knew it," he growled. "I'm dying."

"David, thank you for everything. The list is endless."

"Good night, sleepy lady. Stay off that foot as much as possible until I get here tomorrow. Do you visit Dominic on weekends?"

"No, it wouldn't be fair to the other children if he had a special fuss made over him. Some of the kids go home, but the rest aren't from Las Vegas. David, I—"

"Yes?"

"Just thank you."

"Sher, I want to kiss you so badly, I can hardly stand it, but I'm not going to because stopping with that would be a tough road to go. Understand?"

"Yes."

"And Sher? Thank you for sharing how you feel about Dominic. Like I said, he's a lucky kid. 'Night."

"Good night, David," Sheridan said softly.

She watched as he turned and walked slowly out of the room. The lights in the living room went off, and the front door creaked slightly as he pulled it open.

"See you tomorrow, Sher-eye-dan," he called, causing Sheridan to burst into laughter as he closed the door behind him.

Sheridan waited until she had heard David drive away before she wiggled out of the dressing gown and dropped it onto the floor. With a weary sigh she settled back against the pillow and stared into the darkness.

David Cavelli. It was incredible that out of the throng of people in the casino he would be the one to rescue her from her precarious predicament. No, not really. It was just like David to take matters into his own hands and get the job done. Good heavens, Sheridan thought, she was thinking about David as if she'd known him for ages. But somehow it was as though she had. She had trusted the Voice, opened her hands, and let go of the rope, knowing he would bring her to safety.

And then, as if it were the most natural thing to do, David had carried her halfway across Las Vegas because, as he put it, "Gosh, Sher, your foot hurts!" He had stated, as matter-of-factly as if he were talking about the weather, that since he had caught her as she came flying into his arms, he got to keep her! Just like that! "You're mine, mine, mine," he'd said, and then had proceeded to act as though she was!

Oh, he was crazy! And dear, and funny, and warm. David had accepted her without question when he believed her to be a skimpily clad trapeze swinger; passed no judgment when it appeared she was an unwed mother with a four-year-old son; then shifted gears and decided her career and doctoral degree were a nice bonus.

Dominic had proved to be no spoke in the wheel. David was eager to meet the little Italian boy who shared his last name and had not hightailed it out the door when Sheridan had stated the complexities of her personal life. She belonged to him now, David had said, so he'd turn on his charm to impress the child who was the focus of her existence.

What still disturbed Sheridan was that David intended, for the first time in his life, to lie to his father. He was willing to overlook her lack of judgment and omit it from his report. Her actions at the Big Top would have set Edward Cavelli off on a rampage, demanding her immediate dismissal from the Haven and destroying her chances to adopt Dominic. But David was not going to allow that to happen because . . . because Sheridan was his, and he would protect her from his father's antiquated standards and narrow-minded views.

Who *was* David Cavelli, for heaven's sake? Sheridan knew the Cavelli family was worth millions, had vast holdings across the country and overseas. Was David a wealthy, bored playboy who was viewing his encounter with her as a bit of unusual excitement in his pampered existence? Had he had so much for so long that the bizarre circumstances surrounding their meeting had produced some sparkle in a life he considered dull and monotonous? Was she a new toy, a plaything he'd entertain himself with while in Vegas, and then forget when he went merrily on his way? Finders keepers—for as long as he was here?

But the kiss had been so— No! A kiss was a kiss. A man of David's looks could command and receive affection from any woman of his choosing. It probably never occurred to him that he would be refused, and Sheridan, like the doubtless multitude of women before her, had responded with total abandonment. He had spoken of the lovemaking they would share as if it were a foregone conclusion and as if it would take place as soon as her ankle healed.

"Well, guess what, Cavelli?" Sheridan said, punching her pillow. "It isn't going to happen! I will not be your diversion while you're here. I've said my thank-yous, and that is that!"

With a determined nod of her head Sheridan snuggled down with every intention of going to sleep. But slumber was elusive as the image of David Cavelli danced before her eyes and the memory of his sensuous lips on hers stirred desires within her. At last fatigue won the battle, and she slept.

Sheridan awoke just after nine the next morning—and her first thought was of David. She pushed the distressing, lingering vision from her mind and moved on to thought two: her ankle. Sitting up in the bed, she threw back the blankets and tentatively pressed on the offended limb. The swelling was completely gone, and a large purple bruise was visible. Swinging her feet to the floor, Sheridan gingerly applied pressure to both feet, smiling as she stood erect with no adverse effects. Apparently her ankle had not been sprained after all, but simply solidly whacked. If she avoided bumping the area that was still sore, she'd be in good shape.

In the bathroom Sheridan picked the pink satin costume off the floor with two fingers as if it were contaminated and, wrinkling her nose, dropped it into the hamper. She'd wash it and return it to Janet, along with a stiff lecture on how her friend had taken unfair advantage to plead her case while Sheridan had been half sloshed. Of course, Sheridan had known she'd consumed the wine on an empty stomach, but that was beside the point.

The long, leisurely bubble bath she indulged in was heavenly, and afterward she dressed in jeans and a fluffy pink sweater. The thick mane of raven hair was plaited in a braid that hung down her back. She felt well rested after her harrowing ordeal on the swing, and her large blue eyes were clear and sparkling. A cup of coffee was in order to ward off the slight chill of the house, and Sheridan padded into the kitchen in her bare feet. She had bumped her foot against the edge of the tub, sending a shooting pain all the way to her knee, but if she didn't have one of her klutzy days, it shouldn't present any major problem. David, she supposed, would throw a fit when he saw her sauntering around as if—

David. There he was again in front of her mind. What a pushy Italian! Coffee was a part of her morning routine; David Cavelli was not! Goodness, what would it be like to wake up next to that strong body and have those arms reach out and— Enough already! David would bring her car back, she would issue yet another thank-you, and send him on his way.

While she was waiting for the coffee to drip, Sheridan disposed of the soggy towel that had held the ice and still lay in a heap on her living room floor. At last settled on the sofa with a mug of the steaming brew, she sipped it leisurely. Minutes later the sound of car doors slamming brought her to her feet, and she peered out the front window. David was standing by the curb talking with two teenage boys and she saw him hand each some money. Her car was parked in the driveway with David's behind it. The boys nodded, jumped into a multicolored Jeep, and David started toward the house. He looked handsomely rugged in jeans and a yellow V-neck sweater worn over an open-neck shirt, and Sheridan frowned as she felt her heart start to beat erratically. The man had charisma all right, and so much blatant sexuality, it was ridiculous. Every move, every gesture, was an announcement of masculinity, and Sheridan drew a steadying breath before opening the door.

"Good morning, David," she said. "Come in."

"Hey, what are you doing walking around?" He frowned as he stepped into the living room.

"I'm practically perfect," she said, wiggling her toes.

"I really think you should take it easy and—"

"Coffee?"

"What? Oh, sure. Thanks." He followed her into the kitchen.

Seated at the small dinette set, Sheridan assured David for the fourth time that her ankle was greatly improved. "Thank you for bringing my car back," she said finally. "How much do I owe you for what you gave the boys?"

"Forget it."

"No, I insist on paying."

"Okay. Twenty-five thousand dollars." He grinned.

"Cute."

"I'll bill you."

"David, please, I—"

"Never argue with Italians on Sunday."

"Why not?"

"It has something to do with our metabolism. We use up all our patience by midnight Saturday and have to rejuvenate."

"You're weird."

"And you are gorgeous. I dreamed about you, Sher. You were an angel with wings, and you flew right into my arms. Which is true really. You came out of the heavens, I caught you, you're mine."

"David, I thought I made it clear that you and I are not—"

"Sher, don't be gloomy. Anything is possible when you want it badly enough and are willing to work hard at getting it."

"Work or play?"

"Whew! Low blow. I suppose you think because I'm a Cavelli I just run around having a wonderful time. Not so. This is the first couple of days off I've had in months. My father expects a lot from his sons and gets it."

"I'm sorry. That was rude of me. What exactly do you do?"

"Investments, my sweet. I am trained to know a good thing when I see it. I see you. You are a good thing. Simple really."

"You said you have brothers," Sheridan said. "How many?"

"Five. And the one very chaperoned sister I spoke of. She's married now though. In fact, all the Cavellis are except me. My mother is praying for my decadent soul."

"Seven children. Goodness, your family gatherings must be something."

"A zoo. I love it. There are babies all over the floor. I swear they all look alike. It's a wonder someone doesn't take home the wrong kid. I spoil them rotten and hand them back. I have a great time."

"It sounds marvelous," Sheridan said. "So if you enjoy the home-and-hearth number, why aren't you a father of four or six?"

"It's not that easy, Sher." David frowned. "I get this knot in my stomach and wonder if the woman is interested in me or my money. I got burned very badly about ten years ago by a gal who looked into my big black eyes and saw dollar signs. Since then I've been wary, extremely cautious."

"I guess being wealthy has its drawbacks."

"At times yes. But you're different, Sher. What you want, I can't buy you. Oh, I could foot the bill for your Italian-speaking lawyer, but I can't pay off a court system or bribe an adoption judge. There's no price tag on Dominic, so what you and I have together is real, honest. I've been waiting a long time for you, Sher."

"David, don't." She shook her head. "I really wish you wouldn't talk as though we're about to embark upon the affair of the decade, because we aren't. You'll be leaving Vegas in a few days, and I don't intend sleeping with you in the interim. That was rather blunt, but I don't seem to be able to get through to you."

"I called my brother Paul last night."

"Did you hear a word that I said?"

"Sure. Anyway, I need the name of your lawyer."

"What?"

"I said I could pay for an Italian-speaking lawyer,

but I don't have to. I have a brother who fills the bill. He has to have all the info from your attorney."

"What?"

"Sher, pay attention. Paul can't go to Italy to approach the courts until he knows what has already taken place. He'll get the scoop from your lawyer and proceed from there."

Sheridan blinked to make sure she was actually awake and shook her head slightly. "I don't think I'm understanding this," she said slowly.

"Really? I thought I explained it pretty well." David shrugged. "Paul Cavelli, my brother, is going to Italy to petition the court to make Dominic an American citizen so you can start adoption proceedings here. You, smart and pretty psychologist, better fix up that little kid's head so he can leave the Haven. Otherwise the whole thing will be a washout."

"I—I can't let you do this for me," Sheridan said, her voice a hushed whisper.

"I'm not, Paul is. His wife wants to go visit her family over there anyway. Paul's mother-in-law really bugs him. He'll be glad of an excuse to work. Won't cost you a penny. Want some more coffee? I'm pouring."

"David, why? I mean, you don't even know me and Dominic. This doesn't make any sense."

"I'll meet Dominic tomorrow. And you? Oh, I know you, Sher. Only your name was missing from the image I had in my mind for a long time. Besides, you're making a bigger deal out of it than it is. You need an Italian-speaking lawyer, and I have an Italian-speaking lawyer brother. Elementary, my dear Watson. Paul's sharp. If anyone can pull it off, he can."

A clamor of voices screamed through Sheridan's head as David got up from the table to get the coffee-pot. David had asked his brother to take on Dominic's case and was discussing it as calmly as if someone were picking up a quart of milk from the grocery store, Sheridan told herself. She couldn't accept this kind of gift from David! But, good Lord, if Paul did manage to have Dominic declared an American citizen, the battle was half won. Yet why was David doing this? What did he expect from her in return? If she refused to sleep with him, would he become angry and tell Paul not to bother? Was this all a subtle blackmail tactic to get her into his bed?

"David," she said as he sat back down, "I would prefer to pay Paul for his services. It would take me quite a while, but I could send him something every month."

"Nope."

"Then—then Paul just won't represent me."

"Oh, that's great, Sher. Let your pride stand in the way of Dominic having an opportunity for a real home. I thought you wanted him here with you."

"Of course, I do!"

"Let Paul do what he's damn good at. We all have our specialties in life. You're a psychologist, I'm a whiz-bang investment manager, Paul's a hotshot lawyer, and on it goes. Don't you think Dominic deserves the best chance there is?"

"Yes, but—"

"Good. It's settled. Paul will connect with your lawyer tomorrow. You'll be kept up-to-date on everything as it unfolds. Do you have any cookies or something? I'm hungry. What would you like to do today? As long as you can walk all right, we'll go out. How about playing the slot machines? I love those things."

"David, you make my head spin."

"That sounds sexy. Want me to tell you what you do to me?"

"No!"

"Just thought I'd ask. Forget the cookies. We'll

have a fancy lunch somewhere. We'll stroll in, wearing our jeans, and act eccentric. I do that all the time. People look at you like you must be someone important to have such gall. Cracks me up. Hey, are those tears in your eyes? What's wrong, Sher?"

"David, I can't think or even breathe! You waltz in here and calmly announce you've possibly found a way to solve my problem in Italy, and then invite me to lunch as if nothing major has transpired. Do you have any idea what this could mean to me and Dominic?"

"Going to lunch? No, I'm kidding. Sure, I realize this will overcome a major obstacle in your path. Call it fate. Our meeting at the Big Top, however, was more than that. It was, my Sher, destiny. Let's go to the MGM Hotel and play the slots. There's a great restaurant there too."

"I don't know if—"

"We'll do it just like in the movies." He grinned. "You hang on my arm and bring me luck and I'll call you doll and baby to make it sound authentic. Get your shoes on and we'll go win a bundle."

"Why not?" Sheridan said, throwing up her hands and walking out of the kitchen.

In the bedroom she pushed her feet into her loafers and took a steadying breath. David was like a cyclone! He operated in a whirlwind existence. Sheridan had heard of men like this. Now she had met one, and he was sitting in her kitchen! He was one of the big boys, the power-and-money people. David Cavelli was a mover, a shaker who strode into any situation on his long legs and took charge. He had turned Sheridan's world upside down in a matter of hours, and she was whirling from the impact of his emergence into her sedate, nonvarying day-to-day life.

David was weaving an invisible web around

Sheridan, making her indebted to him beyond measure with his telephone call to his brother. She desperately needed Paul's help, and it was there for the taking.

But what price would she have to pay? What did David Cavelli want from her in return?

Three

The MGM was bustling with activity, and the many enormous twinkling chandeliers that stretched across the ceiling of the casino transformed it into a fairyland. Sheridan and David rode up to the main area on a wide escalator that was banked by mirrors, reflecting their images and the glittering lights into infinity. It somehow reminded Sheridan of David. His mere presence seemed to have a far-reaching effect, the end of which could not be seen.

"Great place, huh?" David said as they walked onto the main floor. "But I suppose you're used to coming to the casinos."

"Not really," Sheridan said. "When I first moved here, I of course wanted to see what the fabulous Las Vegas Strip was all about and spent an entire day roaming from one club to the next. I put a quarter in a slot machine and it gobbled it up, so I decided that was enough of that. Last year after your father's visit a few of us celebrated with a night on the town down here, but that's the extent of my razzle-dazzle."

"My father leaves and you all shout hooray." David chuckled.

"Well, it's very unnerving to feel you're on trial and being so closely scrutinized. I don't mean to sound rude, David, but it was a definite relief when he was gone. Your mother is a delight, but she wasn't in on the individual interviews we had. Just think, this year you get to play king of the hill."

"And not looking forward to it." He frowned. "I made this junket about three years ago with my father and I felt like a potential executioner sitting in that room. My brothers all felt the same way when it was their turn. Definitely not our cup of tea. Come on, let's get some change for the big greens."

Sheridan's eyes widened as David pulled a money clip from his pocket and withdrew several large bills, exchanging them at a booth for trays of silver-dollar tokens. They edged their way through the crowd, and Sheridan was very aware of the appraising glances and dazzling smiles David was receiving from many of the women in their path. He appeared oblivious to the scrutiny, but Sheridan surprised herself by linking her arm through his possessively. David smiled warmly at her.

"Now," he said, pulling over a stool and patting it. "You sit here. I plop in the coins and you pull the handle. As a team we're unbeatable."

"Ha!" Sheridan said, taking her perch. "These things have enormous appetites."

The nonhuman slot machine couldn't have known it was dealing with a Cavelli, Sheridan told herself. It was impossible, wasn't it? Still, Sheridan was soon holding a huge plastic container in her lap that was filled to the brim with tokens the machine had poured out in a steady stream. David had whooped with delight when the coveted sevens had lined up in a row, and he kissed Sheridan enthusiastically. She had to take a shaking breath to regain her

composure after the searing embrace, and David had
to remind her to pull the handle.

For over an hour they were shoulder to shoulder.
Sheridan's senses were whirling with the scent of
David's after-shave, the lingering aroma of soap. The
muscles in his shoulders bunched when he scooped
the coins out of the tray, and she saw how wavy his
thick hair was as it fell just over his collar. His ebony
eyes seemed to glow as he glanced back and forth
between Sheridan and the window on the machine.
Every motion, every gesture, was an announcement
of masculinity, and Sheridan resisted the urge to
reach out and touch the strong arm just inches away
from her.

It was as though her imprisoned sexuality were
screaming to be released, to achieve its potential and
receive into its care what David's maleness was offering. The kiss of the night before had been but a token
of the potential he possessed to awaken her slum-
bering femininity. They were in a crowded, noisy Las
Vegas casino, for Pete's sake, and still desire was
growing in the pit of her stomach, weaving its way
through her body. David exuded sex appeal without
even trying, and it was driving Sheridan crazy.

"Enough and thank you," David said finally,
patting the humming machine. "My stomach says it's
time for food."

"Good idea," Sheridan said, sliding off the stool.
"Heavens, I can't carry this bucket. It weighs a ton!"

"Wait here and I'll go cash it in. Then I'll buy you
the best lunch in the place."

She smiled. "You're on."

Sheridan watched as David lifted the heavy container and walked toward the change booth. A
shapely blond woman stopped him and obviously
made some reference to his winnings as he smiled
and nodded. The woman slid her hand slowly up

David's arm and he bent lower as she whispered in his ear. Laughing, he shook his head and moved away as the woman shrugged and sauntered off in the opposite direction. Sheridan smiled in smug satisfaction. Whatever the blonde had proposed, David hadn't been interested.

This time anyway, Sheridan thought, and frowned. The female population of the world was not made up of idiots. They knew blatant sexuality when it came striding across a room, and there were plenty in the species who would make no bones about wanting to partake in what they saw. But not today. David was with Sheridan Todd, and those women could just keep their greedy paws to themselves!

"All set," David said when he returned. "Money sure is dirty. I'll wash up and meet you at the top of those stairs."

"I thought for a minute I'd have to come rescue you from that blonde," Sheridan said.

"Who? Oh, she was volunteering to help me spend my loot. I told her I had a very jealous wife who packed a twenty-two. That line works every time. See you in a few minutes."

Sheridan washed her hands in the ladies' room and waited for David at the designated spot. She drank in the sight of him as he made his way in her direction, her heart racing as his long strides quickly covered the distance. Her reactions to the man were ridiculous, she decided, shaking her head slightly. She was admittedly overwhelmed by the power he commanded simply by picking up a telephone, but her continual response to his sexuality was getting out of hand! He was a man—no more, no less—and her inner stirrings were absurd. They were also dangerous, and if she didn't get herself under control, she was going to be a goner for sure!

They were seated at a cozy table in the plush restaurant. After they had ordered, David leaned back in his chair, crossed his arms over his chest, and squinted at Sheridan.

"Do you have a problem?" she asked.

"You are so beautiful, Sher," he said. "I saw the men looking you over out there and I didn't like it. Not one little bit."

"Looking at *me*?" Sheridan said, bursting into laughter. "David, the women were drooling over you. Oh, this is silly."

"Gosh, Sher." He grinned. "Do you suppose we're the Couple of the Year?"

"Oh, at least."

"Seriously, I resent even another man's eyes having a part of you. You're mine, Sher, and I swear, if anyone touches you, I'll—"

"David, for heaven's sake!"

"I mean it! And I don't mind telling you I've never felt this fiercely possessive. It's a new emotion for me and I guess I'm not dealing with it very well. But, Sher, you've got to understand that nothing like you or this has ever happened to me before. My mind is going a hundred miles an hour with questions I want to ask you, things about you I need to know. We'll share everything. Nothing will be too small or insignificant."

"David, you confuse me when you talk this way." Sheridan frowned. "You'll only be here for three or four days, and then you'll go back to L.A. We have no time even to say hello, let alone to 'share everything.'"

"Sher, I don't think you understand. Granted, I have to get back to the coast, but only long enough to tie up some loose ends and turn over other accounts to my men. Then I'm taking a long-overdue vacation and returning to Vegas. To you. Us."

"I work all day, David."

"I realize that, but the nights will be ours. I'll be

back, Sher, unless you tell me right now you don't want to see me again. Can you deny that something special has happened between us? When I kissed you last night, it was as though I came out of a lifelong fog. We're here, together, and it's important, special, rare. Do you feel it, Sher?"

"Yes," she whispered. *Oh, Lord,* she thought wildly, *what have I done?* Tell him to go home, Sheridan. Open your mouth and say the words!

"Sher," David said, taking her hand between his large ones, "I'll whiz through this nonsense at the Haven and fly to L.A. as soon as I can. Then it will be just you and me."

"And Dominic," she said softly.

"Hey, I'm not forgetting that little Italian. I'm going to do my charming number on him, remember?"

"David, do you always move so quickly? I mean, you seem so sure that you and I—"

"Am I rushing you?"

She laughed. "You could say that."

"Oh. Well, I'll slow down a bit. I don't want to scare you off, Sher-eye-dan." He smiled.

"I'm not sure I'm taking all this seriously, David."

"You will, sweet Sher, you will. Ah, here's lunch. Steak and lobster. Great! Eat up. It will be good for your foot."

"Of course, Doctor. Everyone knows that."

They chatted comfortably through the meal, David asking Sheridan about her childhood in Michigan; her chosen profession; her favorite color, food, movies, and songs. Big things. Little things. Sharing things. Sheridan relaxed and answered David's questions, the rich timbre of his voice soothing her jangled emotions. He made no further reference to his return to Las Vegas or what it would mean to their relationship. He simply talked, making Sheridan feel as though her opinion on the state of the economy were the most fascinating thing he had ever heard.

She basked in David's attention, acutely aware of how long it had been since she'd received such warm gazes and tender visual embraces. Since Dominic had come into her life, she had kept men at bay, wanting no part of any involvement that would end in heartache when the man wouldn't accept Dominic as her son. Every instinct told her she should be keeping the same distance between her and David, but it was so difficult, next to impossible. David was— Lord, what was he? What place did he want in her and Dominic's life? He continued to speak as if their future together were settled, a closed issue. Sheridan was his, he would revamp his entire work load so he could be by her side, and that was that. Was what, dammit? Sheridan continued to wonder.

Would David return to Las Vegas and assume they would become lovers? Would they live together? Would he camp out in her house or his hotel? Sheridan still had no idea where David thought they were headed. Had she missed a message here? Surely he didn't believe he loved her. No, there had been no mention of the word. They would be together, he had said. Meaning? Lord, he was confusing her so terribly, she couldn't think straight. And supposing she didn't care for whatever status he declared their relationship to have? Would he withdraw the offer of Paul's help? Had she misled David into believing she had agreed to an affair?

"David, I'm not sure we're communicating on the same wavelength," Sheridan said as they sipped one last cup of coffee.

"About what?"

"Us."

"It's clear to me, Sher."

"Well, it isn't to me. I'm sorry if I seem dense, but

you've taken me by storm. You're here to do the annual review of the Haven, and the next thing I know you're talking about an extended vacation."

"How else can we be together?"

"Just what does that word imply?"

He smiled. "That we're not apart."

"David, please! I'm trying to be up-front with you and you're talking in circles. Okay, I'll just spit it out. Are you assuming we'll become lovers when you come back to Vegas?"

"No."

"You're not?"

"Sher, I have three or four days before I even leave! I want you now, this minute, and I can tell from how you responded to me last night that you feel the same."

"But—"

"If you think we should wait until I'm on vacation, then—"

"David, for heaven's sake!"

"Okay, we won't wait."

"David, stop it! You're driving me crazy!"

"I said I wouldn't rush you and I meant it."

"What do you want from me?" Sheridan said, leaning forward. "Just give me a very simple answer."

"You, Sher-eye-dan. I want *you*." He grinned. "Simple enough? But then you're already mine because I caught you in these very arms you see before you. Now I know why Paul is the lawyer and not me. I guess I don't articulate very well. I keep confusing you."

Sheridan frowned. "Did you answer my question?"

"I think so." He nodded. "Yes, I'm sure I did."

"What exactly did you say?"

"That you and I are going to spend every minute possible together. That you and I will become lovers when you feel comfortable and sure the time is right. And that you and I are an incredible happening."

"Oh."

"Let's drive out to Hoover Dam. I've never had the chance to see it."

"Yes, all right," Sheridan said as if coming out of a trance. "The dam is spectacular. You shouldn't miss it." Now she understood what he meant, she thought, getting up from the table. Didn't she? No, dammit, she didn't! What had David said to her? Was *she* now in charge of deciding when they'd go to bed together? Lord, she was slipping over the edge.

"Sher, why are you frowning?"

"It's an early sign of a nervous breakdown."

"You're so cute, Sher. Absolutely adorable."

The weather was warm, the sky a clear blue as they drove to the magnificent structure. Sheridan announced that she would be the cruise director and proceeded to inform a delighted David that Hoover Dam was one of the seven man-made wonders of the world and had been constructed between 1931 and 1936.

"You will notice, sir," she continued as they stood by the water, "that the dam is seven hundred and twenty-five feet high."

"Oh, yes, I caught that right away."

"Which is the equivalent of a seventy-story building, Mr. Cavelli."

"Indeed." He nodded solemnly.

"The base is six hundred and sixty feet thick," Sheridan said, bursting into laughter. "That's the length of over two football fields. Are you impressed with all this great info I have stored in my head?"

"The Chamber of Commerce needs you, Sher. You've missed your true calling."

"I know. I was born to be a trapeze swinger, but I misinterpreted the signals."

"You could be right. You sure looked snazzy in that little outfit you had on. No, forget it. That was a one-night career that lasted long enough for you to tumble into my arms."

"You could have been badly injured, David. Didn't you stop to think before you climbed up on that stool?"

"Not really. Everyone was yelling and running around, but not doing anything, so I just rounded up some big guys and told them the plan. It got the job done."

"You take things by the horn and jump right in, don't you?" Sheridan said as they walked slowly back to the car.

"Sher, in this world there are doers and watchers. I'm a doer, if there is such a word. You have to go by your instincts."

"Do you ever make mistakes?"

"Rarely."

Sheridan laughed. "Goodness, such confidence," she said as David started the car and headed down the road.

He shrugged. "My record speaks for itself. My business investments are money-making endeavors. Big bucks, Sher-eye-dan."

"And your personal life?"

"I told you I blew it once many years ago and learned my lesson the hard way. Since then, no slipups. No heavy-duty involvements either. Until now. Until you, Sher."

"David, I am not one of your purchases that you can check out on a profit-and-loss sheet. Maybe it's been so long since you've dealt in a human situation you've forgotten how to be objective. There are no guarantees that you'll achieve what you've set out to do simply because you've decided that's the way it's going to be."

"I've already done it, Sher."

"David, you're not listening to me!"

"Sure I am. You're saying that you and I might not make it, but that's impossible. We have everything going for us. What can go wrong? Nothing."

"David, be reasonable. We come from different worlds. In actuality we have very little in common. You're a wealthy man from a highly influential family. You operate on an entirely different plane than I do."

"Sher, I'm a man first and foremost. My economic status and last name have nothing to do with anything I'm feeling for you. You're looking for trouble where there isn't any. So I pay more taxes than you do, so what? It's not a big deal. I work hard for what I have, just like you do. Things aren't handed to me on a silver platter. My father has made very certain of that, believe me. We're going to be fine, Sher, you'll see. Trust me a little here."

"Where are we supposed to be going, for heaven's sake?"

"Back into town."

"No! I mean with our lives."

"Wherever we want to. It will all fall into place. We'll just take it one step at a time, but we'll do it together. Right?"

"I don't know, David," Sheridan said, shaking her head. "In all honesty you scare me to death. You're muddling my brain. I had my life all mapped out, and suddenly here you are turning it upside down and backward."

"You just need a little time to adjust. How's your foot?"

"What? Oh, it's fine."

"Listen, why don't I see if I can get tickets to one of those flashy shows on the Strip tonight with all the dancing girls? It will be fun."

"I— Yes, all right, I guess."

"Great. Quit frowning, Sher. You're so pretty when you smile. You are, in fact, the most beautiful woman I have ever seen. Your hair is incredible. Wear it loose tonight, Sher. I want to see it falling down your back where I can sink my fingers into it. It's like an ebony waterfall."

Sheridan swallowed thickly and shifted in her seat as a spiraling wave of desire swept through her. David had not taken his hands off the steering wheel, but she felt as though she had been tenderly caressed. The mere sound of his voice, the seductive words softly spoken, had heightened her passion to an unbelievable level. David Cavelli was consuming her mind and staking a claim on her body, and she seemed powerless to resist him. It was wrong, terribly wrong, Sheridan told herself. There was no room in her life for him. Dominic was her main focus, her reason for being—and nothing would deter her from her goal of obtaining her son.

But yet, since meeting David, she had had her first glimmer of real hope in regard to her and Dominic's future. Because of David's intervention and the willingness of his brother to come to her aid, Sheridan was about to be represented in the courts in Italy by a top-notch lawyer who even spoke Italian. Without David Cavelli it wouldn't have happened. And without him, she would not be experiencing a new, strange, and almost frightening awareness of her femininity. Where was it all leading? She was drawn more and more to David's compelling magnetism, rendered incapable of thinking logically and rationally. Her emotions swung from panic and an urge to run like hell to a swirling mass of tangled desires that were building rapidly into a passionate fire that only David could quell.

Could she have it all? Dominic, David, her career, everything? Oh, how greedy and totally unrealistic, she thought. Choices would have to be made, conclusions reached if she continued to allow David to manipulate her existence. Lord, what a harsh word. He wasn't exactly manipulating her; he was simply being himself—stating facts as he saw them and charging forward with his nonstop energy and drive. If she decided to join him, it would be her decision alone to make. The ultimate verdict would be hers.

"How's this for a plan?" David said, startling Sheridan out of her reverie. "I'll drop you off and call you later and tell you what time I'm picking you up. I'll use this afternoon to go over the reports I need to study before I visit the Haven tomorrow."

"Fine, but I think it would be best if we act as though we've never met when we're introduced at the school."

"I suppose you're right, but it's such a great story. I will, however, be very discreet, sweet Sher. Excuse me, it's sweet Doctor Todd."

"Thank you, Mr. Cavelli." She smiled. "I will politely shake your hand and welcome you to our fine establishment and express the wish that you enjoy your stay in the exciting city of Las Vegas."

"I'm having a wonderful time," he said, chuckling, "and it's getting better every minute."

"You're just saying that because you won playing the slot machines."

"Nope. I'm saying it because I won you, Sher."

"Here we go again." Sheridan laughed. "The Cracker Jack-prize bit."

"No way. You're a valuable treasure that I'll cherish."

"Nicely said."

"Honestly said. That is one thing you can count on, Sher. I'll never lie to you. There isn't room in our relationship for deception. I know, I know; I'm about to hedge on my report to my father about you and the swing number, but that's different. I promise you, I will not phony up on anything I say or do where you are concerned. Fair enough?"

"Very."

"So tell me, how did you ever meet a trapeze gal from the Big Top in the first place?"

"Janet? Her niece is at the Haven with hearing problems similar to Dominic's. We became acquainted and we go to a movie or out to dinner when she's between boyfriends. She's fun. She's a bit of a bubble-head, but refreshing, and she makes me laugh. She talks a hundred miles an hour without coming up for air."

"I bet she doesn't look as good as you do in that costume."

"Janet is a gorgeous blonde. You'd like her."

"Not interested. I have a blue-eyed, raven-haired beauty, and that's all I need. Quit trying to give me away, Sher. You're stuck with me."

"Do tell."

"Yep. I'm yours, which complements the fact that you're mine. It all works out very nicely."

"You're exhausting me, David," Sheridan said, shaking her head. "You have so much energy."

"What kind? Physical, mental, sexual, what?"

"I'll pass on answering that one!"

"Darn. This was just getting good!"

Their mingled laughter danced through the spring air as David picked up Sheridan's hand and kissed the palm. The soft feel of his lips against her warm skin sent tingles of pleasure through her body, and she smiled. David patted the plush seat next to him. Sheridan slid close and rested her head on his upper chest as he circled her shoulders with his arm. His sweater felt rich and lush and comfortable, and she was aware of the rock-hard muscles beneath. The aromas reaching her were masculine and uniquely

David. The after-shave, the soap, the faint scent of male perspiration, were now familiar and belonged only to him.

They rode in silence until David pulled into Sheridan's driveway and turned off the ignition.

"Home safe and sound," he said. "I'll see you in and get the name of your lawyer. Then I'd better do my homework so I don't sound like an idiot tomorrow."

Inside the house Sheridan gave David her attorney's name, address, and telephone number and thanked him again for calling Paul on her behalf.

"My pleasure, ma'am," he said, circling her waist with his arms and pulling her against his firm body.

"I seem to spend a lot of time thanking you for things."

"Which means you must talk too much," he said, then lowered his head and claimed her mouth in a long, searing kiss.

Sheridan seemed to melt as she molded her slender frame to David's hard contours. His tongue explored her sweet mouth with a seductive, rhythmic motion that brought a quiet moan from deep within her throat. His hands slid down over the firm slope of her buttocks, pressing her close to him, his arousal evident as the kiss intensified. Sheridan spread her fingers out like a fan over his back, feeling the muscles move under the increasing pressure she applied. Lord, he felt good. Her body and mind were consumed by the sight, the smell, the very essence of the man. As his lips traveled down her neck she tilted her head back and closed her eyes to savor each moment of the exquisite journey. Their breathing was ragged and heavy, and David shuddered slightly before taking a small step backward.

"Man," he said, his voice hoarse and strained, "I want you so much, Sher. I'd better leave while I can."

"Oh, David."

"I'll call you later." He kissed her quickly on the forehead and walked to the door. She stared after him until he quietly closed the door behind him.

Sheridan sank onto the sofa, her trembling legs refusing to support her for another moment. She rested her fingertips on her throbbing lips as she drew a shaking breath. She had to think! She must get a grip on herself! The sexual tension between her and David had reached an incredible level of intensity in an equally incredible short length of time. They couldn't continue like this. She would have to end things immediately or be willing to succumb to the desires that were raging out of control.

Tonight. Would it have to be tonight, one way or the other? Oh, help! What was she going to do? Say good-bye to David? Never see him again except in his official capacity at the Haven? Or allow herself the luxury of receiving the strength, power, and virility of his lovely body? There was no doubt in Sheridan's mind that their lovemaking would be a glorious celebration. But her future with David was a blur of uncertainties. What he saw as crystal-clear, she viewed as a jumbled puzzle. Could she emotionally handle a brief affair, for in actuality what else could it be? She and David were worlds apart, whether he chose to believe that or not. But she had never, *never* desired a man the way she did him. She ached with the need of feeling his manhood filling her, extinguishing the flame of passion that was enveloping her.

A solid knock at the front door jolted Sheridan out of her tangled thoughts, and she jumped in startled surprise. The insistent summons was repeated twice more before she could answer it.

"Oh, thank God you're not in a body cast or worse," Janet practically shouted, stomping into the room after Sheridan opened the door. "I was just at the Big Top and heard what happened. Oh, Sheridan, do you hate me? Don't answer that. Are you all right? You look all right. Oh, you must have been scared out of your mind. Barney said some hunk of a guy saved your life and Candi was all starry-eyed about a movie-star type that carried—carried?—you into the dressing room and—"

"Would you like some iced tea, Janet?" Sheridan asked calmly.

"Sure."

"Come into the kitchen. How was your camping trip?"

"Grim. There's bugs out there, and I nearly froze to death and I would have killed for a bubble bath. Oh, well, can't win them all. Sheridan, back to the point. Are you okay?"

"Just one bruised ankle to show for my adventure. Oh, I lost your dumb slippers and I haven't washed the costume yet."

"I have others. So who is Mr. Gorgeous? The girls at the casino are all in a dither. Damn, why did I take the night off? I could have been the one he rescued. But no, I was out communing with nature. Sick. Why won't you tell me who the handsome hero is, Sheridan?"

Sheridan laughed. "His name is David, and he's so gorgeous, he's enough to make a woman weep."

"It could have been me! So where is he? You didn't let him get away, did you?"

"He just left."

"Dammit! My timing is lousy. I wouldn't try to steal him, Sheridan. I'd only gawk and drool a bit. He's really yummy, huh? Candi said he looked Italian or Greek. You know, swarthy; the original 'tall, dark, and devastating.' "

"Italian. One hundred percent pure."

"Just like your Dominic! Perfect. Does he like kids? Lord, he's not married, is he? Nope, guys that good usually aren't. They just sleep around the world. When are you seeing him again?"

"Tonight."

"Really? Super! Isn't this exciting? Just like in the movies. So what happened?"

"When?"

"From the minute he caught you when the swing broke up until now," Janet said. "Don't leave out a single detail."

"We went to Hoover Dam."

"That's it?"

"Had lunch."

"And?"

Sheridan shrugged. "He won a bundle playing the slots at the MGM."

"How boring. Oh, I get it, you're not the kiss-and-tell type. I can respect that, Sheridan."

"Janet, really!"

"Italians have heavy-duty libidos, kiddo, and from what Candi said, this guy got his share and then some of sex appeal. Oh, you lucky duck! Is he rich?"

"Very."

"Oh." Janet moaned. "I can't believe this! Is there anything wrong with him? He's got to have a flaw so I'll feel better."

"Not so far," Sheridan said thoughtfully. "David is rather overwhelming, to say the least. You definitely know when he's in the room."

"What are you going to do with him?"

"Do?"

"Yeah, do."

"You make him sound like a fish! Keep him or throw him back in the pond."

"Exactly." Janet nodded eagerly. "You're not going to let him get away, are you?"

"It's not that simple, Janet. In fact, it's very complicated. I have Dominic to consider and Lord, I almost forgot. David has asked his brother to go to Italy and present my case before the courts to have Dominic declared an American citizen."

"David did that after just meeting you?"

"Yes, and Paul, his brother, agreed to do it."

"Heavens, this is a whole new ballgame."

"What is?"

"Sheridan, the man isn't just hanging around to get into your pants! He's trying to help you adopt your son!"

"I know. He—"

"Wow! That is something! The big leagues! We're talking love here. Undying devotion and all that good stuff."

"Janet, for heaven's sake, I hardly know David. Well, I feel as though I've known him for a long time, but he does have a rather unsettling effect on me when he— Do you want some more tea?"

"Oh, boy, you are in trouble, Sheridan. All the signs are there and Darling David isn't exactly playing it cool either. Sending his brother to Italy for you? Lord. The love bug didn't just bite you two, it gobbled you up!"

"Janet, you're overreacting."

"Me? Not guilty. I've got to run. Thank goodness you're all right. And Sheridan? I'm happy for you. Your David sounds wonderful. You deserve the best, cookie, and he seems to fit the bill. Love ya, kid. Talk to you later."

"Bye, Janet," Sheridan said absently. What a cuckoo Janet was, she thought. She'd hardly said three words, and Janet had her head over heels in love with David and vice versa. That was ridiculous! It was also, she decided, not the issue at hand. The problem was the evening ahead with David and the ultimate end it might come to. Did she send him packing or welcome him into her bed? And what about her heart? Could she separate the physical from the emotional? She didn't know. She honestly did not know. The Janets of the world were capable of keeping everything in its proper slot and not confusing things by becoming mentally involved with a sexually gratifying partner. It wasn't particularly immoral. It was practical.

The ringing of the telephone brought Sheridan instantly to her feet and she answered it cheerfully on the second ring.

"I miss you," David said, omitting the usual hello.

"Well, uh, that's nice," Sheridan said, a wide smile spreading across her face.

"I got the tickets and I'll pick you up at eight."

"Fine."

"What are you doing right now?"

"Talking to you."

"Clever. I mean, before I called."

"My friend Janet was here to make sure I was still alive after my ordeal on the swing. You made quite a hit at the Big Top, Mr. Cavelli. The girls are still buzzing about the handsome, dashing hero who saved the day."

"Spare me. What will you do between now and eight o'clock?"

"Oh, write a letter to my folks, read a book, take a long bubble bath—"

"In the nude?"

"That's usually how one takes a bath, yes."

"I'll come scrub your back."

"David!"

"Sher, do you know how boring this report is I'm reading? Maybe I'll just wing it at the school tomorrow and come over to your place now."

"I'll tell your father."

"You probably would. Okay, I'll suffer through it. Bubble bath, huh?"

"Yep."

"You're killing me, Sher."

She laughed. "Good-bye, David."

"Bye, sweet Sher. Remember, wear your hair down. For me."

Sheridan smiled as she heard the dial tone and then slowly replaced the receiver. Oh, yes, she'd fix her hair just the way David had asked her to and put on her prettiest dress and— And what? Say and do exactly what? Why didn't she know herself better than this? Surely at age twenty-seven she should be capable of realizing what she could or could not handle. But her limited experience consisted of one affair of the heart—where the giving of her body had been a forerunner to a lifelong commitment that had ended in a betrayal. She had been young, idealistic, and foolish, and since then no one had kindled a flame of desire within her. Until now. Until David Cavelli. Sheridan suddenly felt unsophisticated, naive, and as if she were floating in a sea of confusion.

She still didn't know what the night would bring, but one thing was certain. Since meeting David, she was already different, changed, and her life would never be the same again.

Four

Sheridan's dress was a teal-blue chiffon that
scooped to the top of her breasts and nipped in at her
waist with a sash. The skirt fell in soft folds to
midcalf, and she ignored the bluish bruise on her
ankle that showed through the pantyhose. Her hair
glowed with the vigorous brushing she had given it
and cascaded down her back in gentle waves.

David's knock sounded just before eight, and she
opened the door immediately. Her greeting was never
uttered as he stepped into the room. She simply
stared at him for a long moment, drinking in the
sight of his perfectly proportioned body in an obviously expensive black suit with a dark tie and a white
shirt. His ebony hair and tawny complexion were
accentuated by the rich fabric, and his shoulders
appeared massive. He was beautiful!

David's gaze roamed over Sheridan's slender figure, then he cupped her face in his hands and kissed
her with lips so soft and sensuous, she thought she'd
dissolve into a heap at his feet.

"Did we say hello?" he asked when he finally lifted
his head.

"I don't think so," she said shakily.

"Hello, Sher. You look lovely."

"So do you, David. Oh, hello."

Even the sound of David's throaty chuckle seemed to assault Sheridan's equilibrium, and she turned quickly to pick up her lightweight evening coat and her purse from the sofa.

"So," Sheridan said brightly once they were driving into the city, "did you study your heart out like a good little Cavelli?"

"I did indeed, including your file, Doctor Todd. I must say, your credentials are most impressive."

"Thank you, mighty master."

"I also read Dominic's history. You've brought him a long way, Sher. The progress he's made since you came to the Haven is phenomenal."

"The teachers taught him the skills, David. I only added the love he was missing."

"An ingredient needed by all Italians, my sweet. We thrive on it."

"Everyone does," she said softly.

"Interesting thought."

"David, why did your grandfather start the Haven? All the children are from low-income families, and there are no fees charged. Is it a tax write-off?"

"My grandfather's sister was born deaf and with a heart defect. Before much could be done to train her in sign language and lip reading, she died. It became a personal goal of his to establish a school where children who might never have the opportunity to overcome their handicaps could receive free services. My father picked up the reins as my grandfather grew older, and now each of us sons takes a turn overseeing the running of the Haven so we'll be prepared to take over."

"I see. Your family has spared nothing. The dormitory rooms are homey, the grounds are kept picture-perfect, the meals are nutritious—"

"And we've hired only the best for the staff."

Sheridan laughed. "You'll give me a swelled head."

"The only problem I can see with the Haven is my father's attitudes. That woman he fired because he didn't approve of her wardrobe was top-notch. It's ridiculous. This Mrs. Alexander who runs the place seems to think just like he does too."

"Oh, she does! I wore my hair down one day, and she said it was unprofessional. Cut it or put it up, those were my choices."

"I'll shoot her! Your hair is—don't get me started."

"The only reason I'm getting away with my personal involvement with Dominic is because of your mother. She's totally behind me in my efforts to adopt him, but Mrs. Alexander doesn't approve of my singling out one child. I'm very careful not to spend excessive time with Dominic since Mrs. Alexander is waiting and watching for an excuse to find fault with my relationship with him. In all honesty, David, working at the Haven is very difficult because of the pressures from the outmoded standards. I really don't think I'd stay if it weren't for Dominic."

"You'd leave Las Vegas?"

"If I had my son with me. There are other excellent schools for him in this country, and I have marketable abilities. I'd like to open my own office someday. But until Dominic is mine, I'm not going to budge. Unless, of course, I step over the line and get myself fired. I live with that fear constantly because it would ruin everything. That's why I'm so grateful you're not going to tell your father about what I did at the Big Top. It was very foolish of me under the circumstances."

"You've got nothing to worry about, Sher. Nothing," David said in a low voice. "We'd better change the subject. The more I think about how my father is running that place, the angrier I get. I have a feeling in my bones that he and I are going to have a wingding of an argument about this one of these days. It won't change anything, but I'll feel a helluva lot better for having said my piece. Someday it will fall into my and my brothers' hands, but until then . . . Enough. I'm getting uptight. I'm not letting anything spoil our evening, sweet Sher."

David had made reservations at the Dunes and the show was an extravaganza. Sheridan thoroughly enjoyed the spectacle that flashed before them in a splendid performance of glittering colors, songs, and dance. Even more, though, she was pleased David held her hand and smiled warmly at her throughout the show.

They shared a quiet dinner afterward, chatting comfortably about many topics. The flame from a small candle in the center of the table sent flickering shadows over the rugged planes of David's face, and Sheridan was aware that her heart was beating erratically more often than not.

As a band began to play, David stood and extended his hand to Sheridan. Within moments she was held tightly in his arms as they glided across the shiny floor. It was heavenly; dancing was a terrific invention, she decided instantly. A perfectly acceptable manner in which to feel the hard contours of David's body, relish the sensation of her breasts pressed against his muscular chest, and savor his special aromas without an eyebrow being raised in disapproval at their actions. She felt the heat from his large hand where it rested on her back and the softness of his lips on her forehead. She would stay in his arms forever if given the choice.

They danced several dances and a rosy glow of euphoria seemed to settle in around Sheridan. David moved with amazing gracefulness for a man his size, and Sheridan felt as though she were floating in the safety of his strong arms.

"Your foot isn't getting tired, is it?" David asked finally.

"A little."

"Okay, Ginger Rogers, that's it for tonight," he said, leading her by the hand back to the table.

"Well, pooh," she said. "I was having a lovely time."

"As was I, my sweet, but that ankle needs to be treated gently for a while."

"I suppose you're right."

"Always, Sher, always."

"Oh, brother!" She rolled her eyes.

"I am not, praise the Lord, your brother!"

Again night turned into day as they walked outside onto Las Vegas Boulevard. The endless row of glittering casinos beckoned to anyone strolling along the sidewalk in the crisp air. David pulled Sheridan close to his side as they walked to the car. As the plush automobile covered the miles to her house Sheridan felt herself grow tense. The moment of truth was just minutes away. Her body was surging with desire after dancing so close to David, and she strove to bring herself under her own command. She had to think clearly, rationally, before they stepped into her living room and she was faced with having to make a decision.

David turned off the ignition when they stopped in her driveway, and Sheridan looked up in surprise. She had been so concerned about cooling her heightened ardor, she had spent no time contemplating what she would do. She handed David her key, and he unlocked the door, stepping back for her to enter.

"It's late, Sher," he said quietly, standing just a few feet into the room. "Maybe I should say good-night now."

"Don't you, uh, want some coffee?" she asked. Oh, Lord, he was going to go, she thought frantically. He was leaving her alone to toss and turn through the long night, needing him, aching for his—

"No, I don't care for any, thank you."

She looked up at him and saw the tight set to his jaw, the fine line of perspiration standing on his brow. Every muscle in his body seemed taut, coiled, as he held himself in check, fighting for control. He averted his eyes from her scrutiny, focusing instead somewhere over her shoulder as he drew a deep, shuddering breath.

"David, I—"

"I said I wouldn't rush you and I won't. I've got to leave now, Sher."

"But—"

"Sher, maybe you're not understanding what I'm saying here. I don't want to do anything that will upset you. I've had you close to me while we were dancing, and my willpower is shot to hell. I'm being honest with you. I really can't handle any more tonight."

A clamor of voices seemed to be screaming through Sheridan's mind. She wanted David to make love to her! She desired him with an intensity beyond description. But what if she lost her heart to this man? What then?

"I saw it, Sher," David said softly. "I saw that flicker of hesitation in your eyes. You're still not sure and I understand that. You'll have all the time you need."

"I—"

"Sher, the purpose, the meaning of my life, is clear to me now. Sheridan, I love you."

"You what?"

"I want to tell you now before we even make love so you won't think I'm saying it in the throes of passion or something. I do love you, Sher, with every ounce of my strength and every thought in my mind. I'll tell you so many times a day, you'll have to believe me."

"But, David, it's so soon, so fast. How can you be certain?"

"Sher, I know! I've waited all my life for you. Now that I've found you, everything has fallen into place. We're going to be happy, you'll see. I promise you, Sher, I'll never make you cry. Never."

"Oh, David, there are so many things standing in our way. And I'm not sure how I—"

"I don't expect you to love me yet, but you will. You *will* come to love me, Sheridan Todd, as much as I love you. We're going to be fantastic together."

"Oh, my," Sheridan said, taking a deep breath. "So much is happening so quickly that I feel as though it's all a dream. I have never known anyone like you, David. You make me feel so incredibly alive and special. You've invoked emotions in me that are . . . almost frightening."

"Don't be afraid. What's taking place is fabulous, wonderful. We're going to have it all, sweet Sher, and when we make love, it's going to be so beautiful."

"Yes. Yes, I know," she said, her voice a hushed whisper.

"Hey!" David grinned. "Let's make love right now on your plushy carpet."

Sheridan laughed. "No!"

"The sofa? Kitchen sink? Will you settle for a boring old bed?"

"David, no," she said, smiling and shaking her head. A rush of relief swept over her as she realized that the tension had momentarily been dissipated.

"Well, damn." He chuckled, cupping her face in his large hands. "I tried. Oh, Sher, believe me when I say I love you, because I do."

David lowered his head and kissed her. Sheridan was immediately aware of the tautness of his body, the slight trembling of his hands as they rested lightly on her cheeks. He was again maintaining a tight control over his desire, and Sheridan felt tears prickle at the backs of her eyes. David was treading softly, pushing aside his own needs to assure that she didn't feel pressured or threatened. Oh, what a man was David Cavelli.

"I'd better go," David said, taking a step backward and drawing an unsteady breath. "I'll see you at the Haven in the morning."

"Yes, all right."

"I know! We'll make love in the bathtub. No, huh? Okay. Good night, Sher-eye-dan. I love you. I love you. I love you."

She smiled tenderly. "Good night, David."

Sheridan didn't move until she heard David's car rumble away from the house. As if in slow motion, she prepared for bed and lay staring up into the darkness.

He loved her. David Cavelli was in love with her, Dr. Sheridan Todd, and the reality, the magnitude of his statement finally seemed to reach her. He couldn't mean it! It had happened too quickly. For all she knew, David fell in love every other week for lack of something better to do. But no, Sheridan told herself, he had been sincere. It would have taken a seasoned actor to invoke the emotion that had been present in David's voice, the warmth and tenderness in his eyes. He did love her!

Sheridan burrowed into her pillow and closed her eyes. She had to get some sleep before facing the long day at the school. But Lord! The most dynamic man she had ever met had just announced he was madly in love with her! She was incapable of sorting out her feelings for him. People who had just encountered a cyclone couldn't be expected to think straight. Would she come to love him in return as he had so confidently stated? Time would tell, and for now it didn't matter. David understood that she was confused by everything that had transpired.

For the moment she would think no further than that she was truly loved, bask in that knowledge, and sleep until the first rays of dawn insisted she face the new day.

"Good morning, Mrs. Alexander," Sheridan said.

"Doctor Todd." The older woman nodded. "You do realize the importance of today?"

"Of course."

"Mr. Cavelli will be arriving within the hour. I expect you to show him every courtesy and give your full cooperation."

"You can count on me," Sheridan sang out as she entered her office and closed the door. A bubble of laughter escaped her lips as she realized the absurdity of the conversation with the director of the school. Cooperate with David Cavelli? You bet your life! And she'd show him courtesy by the bucketful the next time he pulled her into his arms. Naughty. Delicious thoughts, but definitely naughty, Sheridan decided as she sat down in the leather chair behind her desk.

Her hair was coiled into a neat chignon at the nape of her neck and the simple lines of the pale blue linen dress gave her a cool, professional appearance. However, how she was going to get through the very stiff, formal introduction to Mr. Cavelli without breaking into a silly grin was another matter. If Mrs. Alexander thought for one minute that there was anything going on between Sheridan and David, the old battle-ax would go through the ceiling!

Sheridan rested her elbows on her desk and cupped her chin in her hands. The image of David floated before her eyes with such crystal clarity, she felt as though she could reach out and touch him. The memory of the previous night and David's declaration of love brought the familiar surge of desire within her and a warm glow to her cheeks. With a firm shake of her head she brought herself back to the present. She picked up a folder and began working on a psychological evaluation she had done on one of the children. She was soon caught up in her task and was oblivious of the passing of time.

A sharp rap on her door startled Sheridan, and she looked up quickly to see Mrs. Alexander entering with David close behind. David. Sweet, dear, handsome David, who looked magnificent in a steel-gray suit.

"Doctor Todd," Mrs. Alexander said, "this is Mr. Cavelli."

"Mr. Cavelli," Sheridan said, rising and extending her hand.

David moved forward and took Sheridan's hand in his, his dark eyes locking onto hers in a tender gaze. "Doctor Todd," he said, "it's a pleasure to make your acquaintance. I've heard only good things about you."

"You're very kind," Sheridan said, managing a weak smile as she extracted her hand, which was being stroked ever so slightly by David's thumb.

"Mrs. Alexander," David said, "I believe I'll proceed with my update interview with Doctor Todd now. I'll catch up with you later."

"But according to the schedule I arranged for you—" the director started.

"This will work out much better," David said,

flashing one of his dazzling smiles. "If you'll excuse us?"

"Oh, well, of course," Mrs. Alexander said, bustling from the room and closing the door behind her.

"Hello, sweet Sher," David said, coming around the desk and pulling Sheridan into his arms.

"David, someone might come in."

"Shhh. I'm interviewing you," he said, and then kissed her until Sheridan was breathless. "You pass," he said, close to her lips, "except for your hair. Take it down."

"You'll get me fired."

"Good. Then we can spend the day together. I love you very, very much, Sher."

"Last night was—"

"A fantastic evening. Another of which is tonight."

"How nice."

"I love you, Sher-eye-dan."

"You just said that." She laughed softly. "David, I think you'd better let me go. This is very dangerous."

"Let's make love on top of your desk," he said, nibbling on her ear.

"No!"

"The floor? The closet? The backseat of my car?"

"David!"

"Shoot! You mean I have to wait until heaven only knows when?"

"Yes!"

"Disgusting." He smiled, then kissed her quickly and released her.

"You'll live."

"No, I won't! Hey, when can I meet Dominic?"

"They'll go to the backyard to play in an hour. I take my break then."

"I'll meet you out there. Well, I guess I'll go tell

Mrs. Witchy-poo that you are a genius and move on to my next victim."

"If you interview them like you did me, I'll break your nose."

David laughed. "Got it. See you in a while, Sher."

As the hour approached to meet David, Sheridan felt a knot tightening in her stomach. He would be seeing Dominic for the first time, and she was suddenly nervous. This was Dominic, her son, and David's reaction to the little boy was vitally important. David loved her, but what about a four-year-old handicapped child he didn't even know? And Dominic? He was wary of strangers, often becoming hostile and withdrawn when confronted by an unfamiliar face. Would Dominic sense the bond between the two adults and feel that Sheridan had abandoned him too?

The sound of children's laughter reached her ears as she crossed the large porch and stepped onto the lush lawn. David was standing by a tree, his hands shoved into his pockets as he watched the activities. He smiled warmly at Sheridan as she came to his side.

"Nice grass," he said. "Want to make—"

"No."

"Which one is our boy?"

Sheridan looked up at David in surprise, a smile showing in her eyes at his choice of words. She caught the attention of a young woman, who nodded and tapped a boy on the shoulder. He turned and, upon seeing Sheridan, took off in a run in her direction. He flung himself into her outstretched arms and she gathered him to her, filling her senses with his smell—a combination of soap and peanut butter.

"Hello, Dominic. Hello, my love," she whispered into his thick black hair before setting him firmly on his feet. Squatting down, she took Dominic's hands and looked directly at him. "Hello, Dominic," she said.

"Ma," he said, a wide smile on his beautiful face.

"How are you?" Sheridan asked distinctly, forming the question in sign language at the same time.

"Fi," he said, also signing the word.

"Fine?"

"Fi."

"Good. Dominic, this is my friend David," Sheridan said, carefully signing the statement and trying to ignore the nervous racing of her heart.

David hunched down and identical sets of black eyes locked in a stare. David waited as Dominic studied him, a deep frown on the child's face.

Suddenly David lifted his large hands and in perfect sign language that matched his words as he spoke. *"Come stai, Dominic?"* he said. *"Sto benino."*

"You're speaking to him in Italian?" Sheridan whispered. "He doesn't understand."

"Buono," Dominic said, a smile lighting up his face.

"My God," Sheridan said.

David reached into his jacket pocket and withdrew a shiny silver dollar. He held it up for Dominic to see, then placed it securely in the small hand and wrapped Dominic's fingers around it. Again adding American Sign Language to his carefully spoken words, David said, *"Ti do questo per fortuna."*

Dominic beamed. "Thank you."

David extended his large hand and a tiny one was placed in his. *"Diventare amici,"* David said.

Dominic nodded. *"Buono."*

David stood up and extended his hands to Dominic. Sheridan wiped a tear off her cheek as the little boy lifted his arms and allowed David to pick him up.

"See, Sher?" David said, smiling. "All it takes is charm and some good old Italian. This is one helluva kid. Aren't you, buddy?" he said, tickling Dominic's tummy.

"My friend, too, Ma," Dominic said. "Oka?"

"Okay!" Sheridan smiled through her tears. "What did you say to him, David?"

"Only that I was giving him the coin for luck and that I wanted to be his friend."

"He's never taken to a stranger like this before."

"Maybe no one spoke to him in Italian. He understood me, Sher."

"I can see that. David, he didn't speak at all when he came here and when they started working with him it was naturally done in English. He was so young, how could he possibly remember a language he was capable of hearing only as a baby?"

"I don't know, Sher, but it's there. Watch this. *Gelato*, Dominic?"

"*Si, buono,*" he shouted.

"*Si.*" David nodded. "*Or di colazione.*"

"*Buono,*" Dominic shouted again.

David laughed. "Better have some ice cream for my pal at lunchtime. Man, he's neat. I think he looks like me, don't you, Sher?"

"You're both beautiful," she said, her voice a hushed whisper.

"Don't cry, Sher. Dominic will think something is wrong."

Dominic frowned. "Ma?"

"Oh, Dominic, I'm fine."

"Fi?"

"*Si.*" She smiled.

"*Bueno.*" He laughed, his dark eyes sparkling.

"All right, children," the young woman called, clapping her hands. "It's time for class."

"Dominic," Sheridan said, her hands moving in

smooth motions, "you have to go in now. I'll see you at lunch."

"Gelato!" Dominic yelled.

"Yes, we'll have ice cream," she said, smiling.

"Oka," he said, wiggling out of David's arms and dashing off to join the others.

"Arrivederci," David said softly.

"I'm going to cry for a year," Sheridan said. "Oh, David, you were wonderful with him. I've never seen him so enthralled with someone he didn't know. I can't get over him understanding Italian and even speaking it."

"He's superintelligent, that's all."

"Why do you know American Sign Language?"

"All the Cavellis do. My grandfather insisted on it. Maybe it was to keep down the level of noise. No, I'm kidding. It was important to him, just like the Haven is. He wanted us to be able to communicate with those kids who are here because of hearing problems. It all goes back to his strong feelings for his sister."

"It certainly impressed Dominic."

"Nope. It was my charisma. Seriously, Sher, I can see why you love him. He's really something. When he ran into your arms, it was a lovely sight. You're his mother, there's no doubt about it. It will happen too. Mark my words."

"I pray you're right."

"Hey, I did all right for myself. I got a package deal. A beautiful woman and a nifty little kid. What a trio we are."

"David, you are so special. Not many men would—"

"I love you, Sher-eye-dan. *Ti voglio bene.* Today, tomorrow, always. You are mine and therefore so is Dominic. I'd kiss you, but here comes Mrs. Busybody Alexander. Say something that sounds like a psychologist and I'll look grim and nod my head."

All Sheridan managed to do was laugh right out loud. She was rewarded by a stern glance from Mrs. Alexander, who ushered a grinning David off for his next appointment. Sheridan stood alone in the quiet yard, her mind whirling from the encounter between David and Dominic. Was it meant to be? Would she have them both? The man and the boy had established an instant rapport, and they both loved her. And Sheridan? Oh, yes, she told herself, she loved them too. Her heart swelled, and tears flowed down her cheeks.

She loved Dominic. She was *in* love with David Cavelli. A mother for the child. A woman for the man. It was good and right and real. She would marry David, they would adopt Dominic, and live happily ever after. Marry David?

A sudden chill swept over Sheridan, and she glanced up at the sky, surprised to see there was still a bright sun overhead. She wrapped her arms tightly around herself as she thought back over David's declaration of love, his fierce statements of possessiveness. He had never mentioned marriage. They would be together, he had said, he'd love her always. Meaning what? They'd be together during the vacation he planned to take and then whenever he could get away to visit Las Vegas? Did saying that Dominic was now also his mean that David would share his affections with the little boy when it was convenient?

Oh, yes, Sheridan was in love with David Cavelli, and to her that meant a commitment for life. She wanted to bear his children, but what did love represent to David? He had found true love at long last, but would it simply satisfy his emptiness, fill the void for a while, and make it possible for him to move on, once again single, with fond memories?

In a few short hours Sheridan had given her well-protected heart away, and she felt naked and vulnerable. She had left herself defenseless against the heartache she would suffer if David left her. Why had she succumbed to his masculinity and damnable, damnable charm? She should have stayed aloof and cautious as she always had, placing Dominic firmly in the front of her mind. This one time she had answered to her own inner needs and ended up falling in love! Not only had she endangered her own emotional well-being, but Dominic's as well. The little boy had lifted his arms in trust to David. If David walked away, Dominic would suffer the tragedy of abandonment once again. Her earlier ecstasy and joy, her contentment, was swept away and replaced by a shroud of icy misery. Sheridan walked slowly back into the school.

In her office she took out Dominic's file and spread it open on her desk. She carefully documented the child's newfound ability to understand and speak Italian. She added that the discovery had been made through the use of the language by Mr. David Cavelli, who had been visiting the school on official business. She then made copies of the information and placed it in envelopes to be mailed to her lawyer and Dominic's social worker so their matching files on Dominic would be up-to-date.

With a weary sigh Sheridan leaned back in her chair and closed her eyes. Lord, it was incredible. One moment she had been so ecstatically happy and now she was being crushed by a black depression. A sense of foreboding crept in and clutched her heart as two tears slid down her pale cheeks.

Five

Sheridan spent the remainder of the morning observing a classroom through a one-way mirror. Her professional eye was trained on Janet's niece, who was having difficulties adjusting to the environment of the school. A tap on Sheridan's shoulder brought her spinning around, her nose bumping squarely into David's chin.

"Hi," he said. "Having fun?"

"How did you escape again?" she asked, unable to suppress her joy at seeing him.

"I told the formidable Mrs. A. that I felt it would be worthwhile to eat lunch with a member of the staff and observe the children in a relaxed setting. Sneaky, huh? I'm going to dine with you and Dominic. Can they see through that window?"

"No."

"Oh, good," he said, pulling her into his arms and kissing her deeply. "Forget lunch," he added when he lifted his head. "Let's play hooky and—"

"Mr. Cavelli, the very idea! Miss having my *gelato*? Never."

"Dumped for a dish of ice cream," he moaned. "Is

there no justice? Teach a woman a little Italian, and she goes crazy. Want to learn the dirty words? They're great."

"I'll pass."

"Just thought I'd offer. By the way, I called Paul this morning and gave him your lawyer's name and number. He's probably phoned him by now."

"I updated Dominic's file with the fact that he understands and speaks some Italian. I'm mailing copies to my attorney and Dominic's social worker."

"Too slow. I'd better inform Paul about that. He's already making plans to leave for Italy."

"Do all you Cavellis move so quickly?"

"Yep. The Hustle Brothers, that's us. Things don't get done if you sit on your tail, Sher. We finish up one thing, and go on to the next."

"Without looking back?" Sheridan asked softly.

"Forward, Sher. Always forward. Let's go eat. I'm hungry."

Sheridan forced a smile onto her lips and left the room with David, his words screaming in her mind. He completed one thing and moved on, she thought miserably. How much time did he allot for the Sheridan project? He may love her, but wasn't his love only for the here and now? Tomorrow would be filled with his next adventure, challenge, and conquest. She was a fool, but it was too late. If she sent David away now, it wouldn't lessen her heartache. She would hold on tight to whatever time she had with him. But Dominic? He mustn't become attached to David, be shattered by the man's departure. She couldn't allow that to happen!

"David," Sheridan said, "Mrs. Alexander already saw us in the yard. Maybe it would be better if you ate at another table."

"Hey, I'm the big shot, remember? I can do whatever I want. You're only following my orders by eating with me. Besides, I'm looking forward to seeing Dominic again. I'll check him out on some more Italian."

"But—"

"What's for lunch besides *gelato*?"

The large dining room was buzzing with the sound of children's chatter and laughter. To keep a semblance of order the staff sat at the brightly painted picnic tables with the twenty-five young residents of the Haven. Dominic spotted Sheridan and David immediately and waved vigorously as they approached.

"Hello, big boy," Sheridan said, signing the greeting.

"I hungra!"

"Shhh, don't yell, Dominic. David is going to eat with us too."

"Oka. See?" Dominic dug his lucky coin out of his pocket and held it up for David to see.

David chuckled and sat down across from Sheridan, who slid in next to Dominic. Trays of piping hot food were passed out by a bustling crew; lunch consisted of fried chicken, mashed potatoes and gravy, corn, and *gelato*.

"Your ears should be buzzing," Sheridan said to David. "I can see the staff talking about you. Have you been an ogre all morning?"

"Me? Never. I'm a super guy. No one's job is in jeopardy. I'd like to give Mrs. A. the heave-ho, but we're stuck with her. These benches are hard. Why aren't there decent tables and chairs in here?"

"I don't know. The kids don't care, and I guess the furniture's easy to maintain."

"I'll recommend in my report that they be replaced. Watch my father think I'm nuts, but my butt is numb already."

"Ma!" Dominic said, pulling on Sheridan's arm. "Ma!"

"*Che cosa vuoi, Dominic?*" David asked. "What is it you want?"

"You live Ma hou, David?"

"No. I don't live there. Do you?"

"No."

"Why not? Your ma has a nice house."

"David, please don't push him about it," Sheridan whispered.

"I won't upset him, Sher. Dominic, would you like to see your ma's house?"

"No! This my hou."

"Dominic," David said, his hands forming the words, "I'm your friend. I gave you that lucky coin. If you kept it in your pocket the whole time we visited your ma's house, you'd get back here safely."

Dominic frowned and reached into his pocket again for the coin, his large dark eyes glancing back and forth between it and David's face.

"What's your last name, Dominic?"

"Cavelli."

"My name is David Cavelli. That makes us very, very special friends. And that is a Cavelli lucky coin. Nothing happens to Cavellis, Dominic. We stick together. I'm going to go to your ma's house and I want you to come with me. Then I'll bring you back."

"David, don't," Sheridan said, seeing the color drain from Dominic's face.

"When?" Dominic asked, his voice shaking.

"Now," David said. "Right now. Look at the clock. When the little hand is on the two, I'll bring you back here. I promise. Cavellis always tell the truth. Always."

"You sta me?"

"Oh, yes, I'll be right there. I'll hold you so tight

and you won't have a thing to worry about. Your ma will come too."

Dominic looked at the clock, at David, Sheridan, and finally the silver dollar in his hand. Sheridan held her breath.

"Oka," the little boy said, sliding off the bench.

"Easy, Sher," David said quietly, "don't blow it now. Just stroll out casually and take his hand. I'll be right beside you. Steer us past Mrs. A. so I can mumble that we'll be back at two. Smile, Sher; you look like death warmed over."

Although her legs felt like wooden sticks, Sheridan got up from the table and waited while Dominic carefully put his coin in the pocket of his jeans. She and David each took one of the child's hands and started slowly from the room. David stopped long enough to say something to Mrs. Alexander, who stared at him with her mouth open.

Outside, the trio walked toward David's car, but Dominic suddenly halted and gripped their hands tightly.

"He isn't going to do it," Sheridan said.

David reached down and swung the boy up into his arms. Looking directly at him he spoke in Italian. Sheridan guided them to the car as David continued to speak to Dominic, and the child seemed to be mesmerized by the soothing cadence of David's deep voice.

"Get in," David said to Sheridan. "Take his hand the minute I set him down."

Sheridan did as she was instructed and David placed Dominic gently in the center of the plush seat, sliding behind the wheel directly after him.

"Ma?" Dominic said, his lower lip quivering.

"I'm here," she said, grasping his hand. "David, take him back inside!"

David turned the key in the ignition and backed

the car out of the parking space as Dominic scrambled to his knees, an expression of fear on his face.

"David, stop!" Sheridan said, her voice rising.

"Be quiet, Sher. Dominic, where's your coin? Get it in your hand."

With trembling fingers Dominic pulled the coin from his pocket and held it with both hands clutched tightly to his chest, his eyes wide. At the end of the long driveway David stopped the car and pulled off his watch. He slipped it onto Dominic's arm.

"Two o'clock," David said, gently turning the boy's face toward him. "Trust me, my friend Cavelli."

Dominic threw his arms around David's neck and when Sheridan reached for him, he refused to budge.

"Leave him," David said, "I can still drive. Lord, the bugger is strangling me. It's okay, Sher. Let him stay here. He's toughing it out. He's a Cavelli all right. God, what a kid!"

No one spoke for the next few minutes as Sheridan stared at Dominic anxiously. It seemed impossible that this was happening. She had studied every textbook, every case history on problems similar to Dominic's in search of some clue that might unlock the hidden chambers of his inner terrors. David had simply held out his hand, spoken in that same voice that had convinced Sheridan to let go of the rope at the Big Top, and here they were driving away from the Haven.

A strange sensation swept over Sheridan as she looked at the boy, his little arms still tightly circling David's neck. Dominic had turned to David for comfort and reassurance, not her. It had been David he had trusted, David who had broken through the barriers. They looked like father and son with their dark hair and eyes, their tawny complexions and Sheridan suddenly felt lonely.

"He's relaxing a little," David said quietly. "Turn on the radio."

Dominic spun around as the loud music filled the automobile. "Terrible," David said. "Push some buttons, Dominic. I can't stand that stuff. Go on, put your finger down there."

The combination of a little boy and buttons to push did the trick, and the rest of the ride to Sheridan's house was a blaring medley of rapidly changing songs and tempos. David smiled at Sheridan and she managed to return the expression weakly. When David pulled into her driveway, he turned off the ignition, opened the car door, and pulled Dominic into his arms before the child fully comprehended what was happening. They were standing in Sheridan's living room in a few moments and the look on Dominic's face was more curiosity than fear.

"His room is in here," Sheridan said, leading the way.

"Hey, look at this," David said, setting Dominic on his feet and flopping onto the twin bed.

"My ba!"

"This is your bed? Who says?"

"Me! My ba! My hou!"

"Oh? You like it here? Whose toys are those? I want the train."

"No, David. My train!"

"Will you share? Let's play with it together."

"Oka! Oka!" Dominic beamed, stuffing his coin into his pocket and dropping to his knees.

David rolled off the bed and shrugged out of his jacket, then sat down next to Dominic.

"I'll . . . get some sodas," Sheridan said, turning and walking quickly to the kitchen.

With trembling hands she poured the drinks and set them on a tray, stopping to take a ragged breath as she clutched the edge of the counter. She was being so selfish, so childish, Sheridan told herself. She should be rejoicing because Dominic was here where he belonged. But he was with David, not her! They hadn't even noticed she had left the room. Two dark heads had bent over the magical train and nothing else had mattered. *She* was the one who loved him! *She* was his mother! Dominic had come with David and trusted the man to see to his safe return. And if David left them forever, what then? Would Dominic look at Sheridan with accusing eyes and ask what had happened to his Cavelli friend?

"Oh, David," she whispered. "What have you done to my son? And what have you done to me?"

Sheridan sat quietly on the bed and watched as the pair on the floor laughed, talked, and made chugging sounds like human trains.

"Hey," David said finally, tapping the watch on Dominic's arm, "it's time to go."

"No. Sta here. Pla train."

"No, I said two o'clock. You can come again another time if you want to. It's up to you."

"I come Ma hou."

"Good boy. Thank your ma for the nice time and *salutila da parte mia.*"

"Si," Dominic said, jumping to his feet and kissing Sheridan noisily.

She smiled. "How nice."

"I told him to give my love to you, Sher. Hence the sloppy kiss." David chuckled. "Okay, gang, let's head 'em up and move 'em out."

The ride back to the Haven was a repeat performance of the button-pushing routine, then after hugs and kisses Dominic was whisked away by an attendant for his afternoon nap.

"A good day's work, wouldn't you say, sweet Sher?" David said.

"I can't believe it, David. You did it. All of it."

"It doesn't matter who was responsible, Sher. The fact remains that Dominic left the Haven and didn't come unglued. I'm going to call Paul right now and tell him to get his tush to Italy. Dominic is ready to come home! I'll see you later."

Sheridan went into her office and once again documented Dominic's file with the latest occurrence. After making copies for the lawyer and social worker, she decided to telephone them with the glorious news, but neither of them was in.

It had been like a miracle. Dominic had sat in his own room in Sheridan's home. It was a moment she had prayed for, fantasized about, and it had happened! David had charged in, taken control, and done it. Want Dominic at your house, Sher? Here. Have a kid. Nothing to it. Easy as saying Cavelli.

How could she possibly find fault with what David had done? His actions had been well intended and the outcome fantastic. Today. For now. But dammit, what did the word *tomorrow* mean to him?

In spite of the tangled web of thoughts in her mind, the afternoon passed quickly for Sheridan as she once again observed a classroom and then held a counseling session with a ten-year-old boy who had recently lost his sight in an accident. At five o'clock she went in search of Dominic to say good-bye, only to find him swinging with David in the backyard. The two were once again imitating trains, and Sheridan smiled as she approached.

"Which one of you is the little boy?" she asked.

"Come swing," David said.

"No, thanks. Dominic has to wash up for dinner and I'm going home."

"You're no fun, Sher. Okay, kiddo, off you go. I'll see you tomorrow."

"Oka, David," Dominic said, raising his arms for

a hug after jumping off the swing. David held a giggling Dominic high in the air, then flung him over his shoulder like a sack of potatoes. Squealing with delight, Dominic was carried to the porch and set on his feet. Sheridan kissed him and said she'd see him in the morning.

"Bye, Ma. I hungra," he said, dashing for the door.

"Me too. Let's go out to dinner, Sher," David said.

"Will you follow me home so I can leave my car?"

"Sound plan, smart lady. In fact, I'll give you a head start. I want to look over a couple of more files before I leave here."

"Fine. I'll see you at the house."

"Kiss me good-bye."

"Nope. Ta-ta," she said, waggling her fingers at him.

At home Sheridan used the extra time to shower and brush her hair into an ebony cascade that flowed down her back. The way David liked it. He would stride into the living room, take her into his arms, and kiss her until all the doubts and fears vanished and she was living only for the moment.

Sheridan dressed in a long-sleeved, kelly-green silk dress, and medium-heel sandals. A thud against the front door announced the arrival of the evening paper. Sinking onto the sofa, she opened the newspaper and glanced at the headlines before her gaze traveled to the center of the front page.

"My God," she gasped, sitting bolt upright. "Oh, no! No!"

There in all its glory was a picture of Sheridan being caught around the waist by David, who was standing precariously on his stool at the Big Top. Sheridan's eyes widened in horror as she saw how her breasts pushed above the top of the costume and the great expanse of her thigh that was visible. Whoever the photographer had been, he was good. Both her and David's faces could be clearly seen, and her outfit allowed a whole lot more of her to be clearly seen.

Sheridan quickly scanned the caption beneath, which stated that a tragedy had been avoided at the casino by the fast actions of the man shown, who had saved the trapeze swinger from tremendous injuries. The reporter had been unable to obtain the hero's name, but the lovely employee of the Big Top was named Sherry. The Big Top was offering a reward to the courageous gentleman if he cared to step forward and claim it.

"Oh, my God, the front page!" Sheridan said, getting up and pacing the floor. "I'll sue. They can't do this to me! They already did! Oh, Lord!"

The sound of David's car pulling into the driveway sent Sheridan racing to the door and flinging it open.

"Hi, Sher-eye-dan," David called as he approached. "Are you that eager to see me? Great!"

"David, hurry. Oh, this is awful."

"What's wrong, babe?" he asked, coming into the house.

"Look!"

David took the newspaper and quickly read the caption after scowling at the picture. He let out a long, low whistle and shook his head. "Not good," he said. "In fact, very bad. It doesn't give our names, but there's no doubt that it's us. Dammit to hell! How did the jerk get this?"

"What are we going to do?"

"Hope Mrs. Alexander doesn't know how to read."

"David!"

"Hey, maybe I'll go see what the reward is."

"Go ahead and laugh. It's not your job that's on the line, Mr. Cavelli," Sheridan said angrily.

"I'm sorry, Sher. I'm just trying to get you to relax a little. The damage is done. All we can do now is wait and see what the ramifications are. It's not that hot of a story to go on the wire service and hit the L.A. papers, where my father will see it. Our chief concern is right here with Mrs. A. She resents the hell out of your relationship with Dominic. That came across loud and clear today. She's after your scalp, Sher. We can only hope she doesn't see this."

"And if she does?"

"I don't know. The problem is, she'll recognize me in this picture too. Otherwise, she might just report it to me and I could say I'd handle it. The way it stands, she's liable to go straight to my old man."

"Oh no," Sheridan whispered.

"Well, what's done is done," David said, tossing the paper onto the sofa. "Now we sit and wait."

"I can't believe this! It was such a wonderful day with Dominic coming here and now—"

"Try to put it away for a while, Sher. Let's just go have a quiet dinner and unwind. I'll tell you one hundred and thirty-five times how much I love you."

"In English or Italian?" she asked, managing a small smile.

"Some of each for variety."

"The spice of life?"

"I used to think that, but not anymore. I am now, sweet Sher, a one-woman man. You're all I need."

"And Dominic?"

"That is one class-act kid. What he did today took more courage than some men possess. Besides, he makes a great noise like a train. He's a good chugger. If I play with his train, will you promise not to tell him?"

"I'll think it over."

"You're a hard, cold woman, Sher-eye-dan. Come on, I'm starving to death. Say, want to wander through the Big Top and see if anyone asks for our autographs?"

"Want a broken arm?"

"Oh."

The restaurant was small and cozy, and David ordered an expensive wine as soon as they were seated. The food would be delicious, he declared, because who'd dare serve anything less in an establishment located on Paradise Road?

"How did you find this place?" Sheridan asked.

"I get around."

"Oh, I bet you do." She laughed. "You even march into women's dressing rooms if the mood strikes."

"Wasn't that fun?"

"Candi thought so."

"Darlin' Candi? Not my type. Her hair was bleached and the eyelashes were false."

"You noticed?"

"I have a trained eye, Sher. Fast and observant. Am I getting myself in trouble here?"

"Deeper and deeper. Keep talking."

"I plead the Fifth."

"Coward."

"Smart coward. Oh, I had a long conversation with Paul. He said the news of today was great and said to tell you congratulations on having your boy pay his first visit home."

"You did it, David."

"Whatever. Anyway, Paul talked with your lawyer, and your guy is delighted with the changing of the guard. Paul is flying to Italy early next week. His wife and five monsters will join him that weekend."

"My gosh, he's not wasting any time."

"Cavellis don't mess around. I thought you knew that by now."

"Paul has five children? How old is he?"

"Thirty-six. One year older than yours truly here."

"Do you look alike?"

"We all do. We wore name tags as kids so our parents would know who we were."

Sheridan laughed. "You're so full of bull."

"I know, but I'm lovable."

"Did your brothers and sister all marry Italians?"

"Yep. That's why all the babies look like reruns. Picture a room loaded with Dominics. Black hair and eyes, dark complexions. Gosh, are Cavellis boring!"

"You're gorgeous."

"Whew. I was getting worried there for a minute. And you're beautiful, so we're a great pair. Beautiful you, gorgeous me."

"Who are presently on the front page of the paper." Sheridan frowned.

"That subject is taboo. Blank it from your mind and concentrate on me. Also give thought to the fact that when I take you home, I am going to kiss you for sixteen hours. No one else but the two of us will exist. We'll close the door on the world and focus only on each other."

Sheridan couldn't breathe. Something just stopped as desire swept through her body. David's words were caressing her, stroking her as gently as if they were his strong hands. She finally drew a shaking breath as David continued to gaze at her with his fathomless dark eyes.

"I love you, Sher," he said softly. "The sight, the feel, the very essence of you fills me up. You're all I need. You are mine."

"David, I—I love you too," Sheridan said, her voice a hushed whisper.

"What? What did you say?"

"I love you. I know that now."

"Lord, Sher, if we weren't in this restaurant, I'd—

You love me? God, I'm the luckiest man in the world. My lady loves me!"

"Would you care to order?" a waitress said.

"Sher loves me," David said happily.

"That's nice." The woman nodded. "Want some dinner?"

Whether they were interested or not didn't seem to matter as David told the wine steward, the busboy, and the parking lot attendant that Sheridan loved him. She just blushed her way through his nonsense and then snuggled next to him in the car as he drove to her house. Inside the living room David instantly pulled her into his arms and kissed her deeply as Sheridan leaned into his embrace.

"Let's call up the world and tell them you love me," he said, his mouth close to hers.

"Let's not."

"I love you, Sher. Oh, how I love you."

She knew. In that glorious instant everything fell into place and was so right, it seemed impossible to Sheridan that there had ever been any doubt in her mind. She wanted this man, this David Cavelli, and she would not regret her actions. Not ever. The tomorrows could bring whatever they would, but tonight was theirs.

"I love you, David, and I desire you so much."

"Sher, are you sure? Have you thought . . . ? My God, you're saying so much to me with those beautiful blue eyes of yours, but I have to hear it. Say the words, Sher. Tell me you want me to make love to you."

"I do, David. Love me. Now. Tonight."

With a moan that seemed to come from his very soul, David pulled her roughly into his arms and claimed her mouth in a punishing kiss, thrusting his questing tongue into the sweet darkness of Sheridan's mouth. She circled his neck with her arms, sinking her fingers into his thick hair, urging him closer and not caring that the kiss was almost painful in its intensity.

"Oh, Sher, I'm sorry," David said huskily. "Did I hurt you? I didn't mean to be so rough."

"No, no, you didn't hurt me, David. You make me feel . . . I can't even begin to tell you. It's as though my femininity were sleeping until you touched me and now I'm awake. I do want you so much."

David reached out and snapped the lock into place on the door, then turned off the light. The moonlight filtering through the drapes bathed the room in a silvery glow. Circling Sheridan's shoulders with his arm, he led her into the bedroom and threw back the blankets on the bed. He turned immediately to kiss her once again with whisper-soft gentleness. His hand drew down the zipper of her dress; he brushed it away from her shoulders and it fell at her waist, where it was caught by the sash.

Sheridan stepped back. The moonlight flickered across her pale skin as she undid the tie and stepped out of the dress. David's breathing quickened as he watched her drop her bra to the floor and then bend over to pull away her shoes, pantyhose, and bikini panties. She straightened again, her eyes meeting his steadily as she stood before him in naked splendor.

"Oh, Sher, you are so beautiful. Even more than I imagined."

With hands that were visibly shaking, David shrugged out of his jacket, pulled his tie free, and reached for the buttons on his shirt. Sheridan halted his motion by the touch of her fingertips. She undid the buttons herself and tugged the material from his pants. His shirt joined her clothes on the floor. With featherlike kisses she traveled over his glistening torso, her tongue drawing lazy circles on the curly black hair.

"Sher, God, you're driving me—" David started, only to take a ragged breath as he reached for the buckle on his belt.

At last he was free of the remaining barriers that stood between them, and Sheridan drank in the sight of David's magnificent body. His manhood announced the urgency of his need, and she inwardly rejoiced that she had brought him to such heightened passion. They moved to the bed, where David stretched out next to her, not touching her for a moment as he struggled for control. Sheridan placed her hand on his rugged cheek and he lowered his head to find her mouth.

The languorous journey began as lips and hands roamed, discovering mysteries and joys, anticipating what would be theirs. Sheridan etched indelibly in her mind each of David's steely, corded muscles as she trailed her hands across the taut surface of David's stomach and beyond.

David's touch sent her swirling in a wave of desire, and she gasped as his mouth found the rosy bud of her breast and drew it into his mouth. The other ivory mound received the same loving attention until Sheridan was writhing under the maddening onslaught, a moan escaping from deep within her throat. When David's hand slid to the soft flesh of her inner thigh, she could bear it no longer.

"David, please. Please."

David answered her plea by moving over her and entering her willing body. She arched her back to meet him, to bring closer the thrusting manhood that filled her. Her rhythmic motions matched his perfectly as the tempo increased and they soared higher and higher away from reality. And then, in an explosion of ecstasy that defied description, Sheridan burst upon an unknown shore. She called to David, gripped his shoulders tightly, and as he shuddered above her she knew he had joined her in that private place.

Slowly, slowly, they drifted back as their bodies cooled and heartbeats quieted. David moved gently away, pulling Sheridan close as he brushed the hair from her face and drew his fingers through its silky length.

"You are wonderful, Sher," he whispered, "and truly, truly mine now. I will never let you go."

Much later, Sheridan lay close to David, listening to his steady breathing as he slept. He had made no mention of going back to his hotel, and she relished the thought of waking up next to him in the morning.

As sleep claimed Sheridan she refused to think. The image of the newspaper that still lay on the sofa flashed before her eyes, and she willed it from her mental vision. Tonight she was safely held in David's arms. Tomorrow . . . oh, the hell with tomorrow! she thought fiercely, and fell asleep.

When Sheridan awoke to the shrill signal of the alarm clock, she shut it off and turned to reach for David. The empty expanse of the bed next to her brought her instantly alert, and she sat up and looked quickly around the room. David's clothes were gone from where he had hastily discarded them on the floor. Her eyes came to rest on a piece of paper leaning against the mirror on her dressing table, and she hurriedly retrieved it. The note read:

Sher,
        Lucky for you I was sneaking out and not in. You sleep like a dead person. I love you, my Sher.

D.

"Damn," Sheridan said, heading for the shower. "So much for breakfast in bed."

At the entrance to the school Sheridan took a deep breath before pulling open the door. If Mrs. Alexander had seen the newspaper— Lord, the thought was too horrible to comprehend. The fact that David's car was already in the parking lot did little to ease Sheridan's apprehension. He wasn't due to arrive for at least another hour. Something was definitely wrong.

"Sheridan," the secretary said the minute she stepped inside, "Mrs. Bitch wants to see you right away."

"Okay, Pat." Sheridan sighed. "Is Mr. Cavelli with her?"

"Yes, but I wish he were with *me*. I have never in my life seen such a fantastic-looking guy."

"He's something, all right," Sheridan said absently as she started down the hall.

A crisp "Come in" acknowledged Sheridan's knock on the director's door, and Sheridan walked in, her gaze immediately coming to rest on the newspaper spread out on the desk. She looked quickly at David, who was leaning against the far wall, his arms crossed over his chest and a stormy expression on his face.

"Sit down, Doctor Todd," Mrs. Alexander said, "although you won't be staying long."

Sheridan sank into the chair opposite the desk, her heart racing as she clutched her hands tightly in her lap.

"I telephoned Mr. Cavelli at his hotel and asked him to be present for this meeting," Mrs. Alexander said. "I'm sure it will come as no surprise to you, Doctor Todd, when I say that after this disgraceful display, which has been paraded through every home in Las Vegas on the front page of the newspaper, your services are no longer desired here at the Haven."

"Now wait just a damn minute," David said,

pushing himself away from the wall. "You don't own this place. It's Cavelli property, and I'm a member of that family, in case you've forgotten."

"Perhaps the black sheep," Mrs. Alexander said coolly. "I recognize your picture here, too, Mr. Cavelli. The whole affair is scandalous and unacceptable to the reputation of this school."

"Mrs. Alexander," Sheridan said, "you don't understand. I was merely doing a favor for a friend that night at the casino. I admit I didn't use the best judgment, but it has no reflection on my ability as a psychologist."

"Everything you do reflects on the Haven," the director said. "You will vacate your office immediately."

"Hold it, lady," David said. "You're overstepping your authority."

"The order comes, Mr. Cavelli, from your father, whom I spoke to on the phone before your arrival."

"You what?" he roared.

"He wishes me to inform you that you are to return to Los Angeles at once. As for Doctor Todd, under your father's directive she is no longer a member of this staff."

"Damn you!" David shouted. "Why? Did you get some kind of perverted pleasure out of destroying Sheridan's job?"

"She did that quite nicely on her own," Mrs. Alexander said, tapping the newspaper with her finger.

"You lousy—"

"David!" Sheridan said, getting to her feet. "It's no use. It's over."

"No, dammit, it's not! I'm not sitting still for this, Sher. They're not tossing you out like a piece of dirty laundry! You're not leaving here!"

"David, your father—"

"The hell with him! I'll fly over right away and have this out with the great Edward Cavelli. You stay put."

"But—"

"You listen to me, lady," David said, leaning forward on the desk and talking close to Mrs. Alexander's astonished face. "Sheridan isn't moving until I get back. In the meantime don't you even say hello to her, understand? She's invisible where you're concerned. You look at her wrong and you'll answer to me. Got it?"

"Yes. Yes, of course. I—"

"Good. Come on, Sher. I can't breathe in here."

David left the office and strode down the corridor so rapidly that Sheridan had to scramble to keep up with him. They entered her office and he slammed the door behind him, taking a deep breath as he strove to bring his raging anger under control. With a bitter-sounding laugh he shook his head, then walked to the window as Sheridan stared at him anxiously.

"It was a great performance," he said quietly, "but worthless. I can't beat him, Sher. All I did was buy you a little time to be with Dominic until I can figure something out. I'm sorry."

"It's my fault, David."

"I am a thirty-five-year-old man, for God's sake," he said, spinning around, his jaw tight as a muscle twitched in his neck, "and I can't protect the woman I love from my own damn father. He's ordering me home like a naughty little boy and tossing you out. I'll go to L.A., Sher, but only to tell Edward Cavelli to go to hell."

"David, no! You can't. Don't throw away your relationship with your father because of me! You'll never be able to live with yourself. You'll come to hate me because of it. Please, David, you're not thinking clearly."

"Oh, Sher." He pulled her roughly into his arms. "I hate this. I never want to see you hurt and I'm powerless to stop it. But I'll try. I'll go to my father and quietly and calmly explain everything. But I swear to God, Sher, if he won't listen, I'm going to—"

"David, please."

"Stay here just like I said. Go through your normal day and ignore that old bat. I'll call you from L.A. tonight. I love you, Sher. Don't forget that."

Tears spilled over onto Sheridan's cheeks as David kissed her deeply. He held her tightly for a moment before backing away and walking out of the room. Sheridan sank into a chair and covered her face with her hands, giving way to the sobs that racked her body. Finally there were no more tears to shed, and she wearily pushed herself to her feet. She went into her small bathroom and splashed water on her face, then stared at her reflection in the mirror.

It was a nightmare. Her world had come crashing down upon her and she felt desperately alone. David was going up against the king, the ruler of the Cavelli empire, and the battle was lost before it even began. Father and son would rage at each other in anger because of her. And Dominic? How would Sheridan explain that she could visit him only during the designated hours once she left the Haven? And what if Mrs. Alexander refused to allow her to see him at all? Lord, no! She couldn't lose her baby, her son! David would think of some way out—or would he? Once home and away from her, would he decide he had made a mistake and wash his hands of the whole mess? Did the tomorrows that he had never defined in their relationship stop, cease to exist, at the first sign of trouble? Just how much power did Edward Cavelli have over his son?

"Oh, David," she whispered, "I do love you so much and I know you love me. But will it be enough? Will it, David?"

Six

Sheridan moved through the morning in a numb blur. When it was time for her to meet Dominic on her break, she moved toward the child with heavy steps. Somehow she would have to explain why David was not there as he had promised he would be. Sheridan dreaded seeing the pain, the betrayal, that would very likely be evident on the little boy's face.

When she stepped off the porch, she immediately saw Dominic running round in a circle, his arms spread out as he made a loud roaring noise. Sheridan managed to gain his attention as he raced past and smiled at her.

"Hi, Ma. I pla," he said.

"A plane?"

"Yes. David go on bi pla in the sky."

"David told you that?"

"Yes. Ma, David come back and bring me pri."

"He's bringing you a surprise? That's wonderful."

"David my Cavelli friend," Dominic said, and roared off across the lawn, flapping his arms.

Sheridan sank onto the bench and watched Dominic buzzing around the yard. David, in spite of his anger and upset, had found Dominic and told the boy he was going on a big plane and would return with a surprise. Sheridan could picture it so clearly in her mind. David would have simply looked Dominic squarely in the eyes and, signing as he spoke in that soothing voice, explained the facts. Dominic had immediately believed, trusted, and accepted the information with no reservations. It had been a marvelous gesture on David's part to see to Dominic's well-being while he himself was so emotionally distraught. The situation was momentarily under control—very momentarily. Sheridan felt as though she were sitting on a loaded keg of dynamite that could explode into chaos at any second.

Sheridan managed to get through the day. She ate lunch with Dominic the airplane and avoided any contact with Mrs. Alexander. The word had spread like wildfire through the staff regarding the events of the morning, and there were mixed reactions. Some of the faculty approached Sheridan to express their dismay and sympathy, while others avoided her as if she had the plague. At five o'clock Sheridan kissed Dominic good-bye and he zoomed into the school for his dinner.

At home Sheridan stood under a hot shower and allowed the water to beat against her weary body. She was physically and emotionally drained, exhausted, and hardly had the strength to hold the dryer and brush her heavy mane of hair. Dressed in jeans and a sweatshirt, she consumed a bowl of cereal and then sat down in the living room to wait. David had said he would call, so he would call.

The evening crept by slowly as Sheridan attempted with no success to read a mystery novel. Her glance continually fell on the telephone, willing it to ring and bring the sound of David's deep, rich voice. By midnight she was a mass of jangled nerves.

She prepared for bed and lay staring at the ceiling, every muscle in her body aching from tension.

"Thank God," she said when the telephone shattered the silence at twelve thirty. She ran to answer it, gasping her hello.

"Sher?"

"Oh, David," she said, sinking onto the sofa. "I've been so worried about you. Did you see your father?"

"Yeah. It's a wonder you didn't hear the lovely exchange all the way over there. My resolve to stay calm lasted approximately three seconds. *Non riesco a fare nulla di quell'uomo.*"

"What?"

"Aren't you listening to me?"

"You were speaking in Italian!"

"I was? I'm so bummed out, I don't know what I'm doing. I said, in essence, I couldn't do a thing with the man. He is the most stubborn, narrow-minded—"

"I'm fired," Sheridan said softly.

"Yeah, babe, and I'm so very, very sorry. I've never been so angry and frustrated in my life. I walked out, Sher. I just turned my back on Edward Cavelli and split."

"Oh, no!"

"All hell has broken loose over here. My mother is frantic, pleading with me to go back and apologize to my father, but it'll be a cold day in hell before I do that, believe me. The only thing I got for you was the right to visit Dominic. They can't keep you away from him, Sher."

"Thank heaven. But what about you and your father? David, you can't allow what I did to come between you."

"Don't worry about it. Listen, I've been holed up with Paul for a couple of hours. He agrees with me, Sher. You've got to get Dominic out of the Haven. I don't trust that bitch of a Mrs. Alexander. There's no telling what she might say to Dominic when you're not around."

"I can't just snatch him up and carry him out the door!"

"Dominic is a ward of the state of Nevada. Paul says that if you can be named his temporary legal guardian while the adoption is pending in court, you could remove him at your discretion."

"But how?"

"Paul and I are meeting with a judge in closed chambers tomorrow morning. The old gentleman's name happens to be Cavelli."

"But your father will be furious if—"

"Judge Cavelli is my father's brother, my Uncle Vincente. I called and filled him in. He's laughing in his wine to think I stood up against Edward Cavelli. They've never gotten along. It's our only hope, Sher."

"David, you can't do this. It's splitting your family apart!"

"Sher, please. I'm so exhausted, I can't see straight. Just trust me that I know what I'm doing. Go to the Haven tomorrow and clear out your desk. You'll have to convince Dominic you're not deserting him. You can still eat lunch with him as you usually do. I checked on that before I left."

"And you spoke with Dominic. He turned into an airplane."

"Gave up chugging like a train, huh?"

"David, I love you so much."

"And I love you, Sher. I really do. I've got to go before I fall on my face. I'll call you tomorrow and give you the verdict on what Uncle Vincente says. He's a tough old bird. If there's a legal way to name you Dominic's guardian, he'll find it. Good night, my Sher. *Ti voglio bene.*"

"I love you, too, David. Good night."

Sheridan drew a steadying breath after slowly

replacing the receiver. If only, only it was just a bad dream from which she could escape. She, Sheridan Todd, was ripping apart a close-knit, loving Italian family. She was destroying the relationship between David and Edward Cavelli, pitting son against father, causing immeasurable grief to Rosalie Cavelli. Paul would no doubt feel the brunt of his father's wrath when Edward discovered Paul had come to David's aid. What had she done? One foolish moment in her life at the Big Top was having horrendous effects beyond her comprehension.

David was angry and tired, and Sheridan feared he was not thinking clearly. She was sure that the reality of his actions hadn't yet filtered through his frustration and fatigue. He would sleep now and wake to face what he had done. Would he swallow his pride and apologize to his father for his harsh words and accusations? He had to! But if he did, would he also agree to give up his quest to have Sheridan named Dominic's guardian? If David gave up the fight and left her to function alone, she would never be able to adopt Dominic. Paul would cancel his trip to Italy, and as an unemployed single woman she would stand no chance of convincing a court of law she could provide a home for her son. Everything would be lost, including the man she loved, David Cavelli, her Cavelli friend, her life and love, the essence of her being.

As though her subconscious knew she could bear no more, Sheridan fell instantly asleep when she crawled into bed. Vivid dreams marred her slumber as haunting pictures of David and Dominic invaded the dark oblivion. Each seemed to be growing smaller, retreating from her view and grasp, until they disappeared entirely, leaving only a lonely void. Sheridan awoke with a sob and lay huddled in misery until the first rays of dawn streaked across the room.

By the time she arrived at the Haven, she had formulated a plan in her mind. Until she heard from David regarding the outcome of his meeting with his uncle Vincente, she would tell Dominic nothing. She would simply appear in the schoolyard during what would be her usual break time, show up again to eat lunch with him, and come back at five to kiss him good-bye. None of the meetings would be against the visiting policies of the school, and Dominic would have no way of knowing that she no longer worked there. If Mrs. Alexander did not tell the boy of the shattering changes, he could be left in the dark for the present.

Sheridan packed her belongings from her office and made several trips to her car with the boxes. Mercifully she saw no one as she completed her task. Tears continually blurred her vision as she worked and she brushed the moisture angrily from her cheeks. She was so tired, needed so desperately to feel David's strong arms around her. Desire surged through her body as she thought of the lovemaking they had shared. She ached with wanting him, her breasts growing taut at the memory of his tantalizing touch.

How she loved David, would always love him, Sheridan thought. She wanted to share her life with him, forsaking all others and standing fast through the good times and bad. Forever.

But David? He spoke of their tomorrows, said he would never let her go, that they would always be together. But he had never mentioned marriage nor referred to her as his future wife. How did he perceive their relationship? Was she simply to assume they would be married? No, David always said exactly what he was thinking. It was all so confusing! Just what role did David picture her playing in his existence?

"I just don't know where I fit into David's world," Sheridan said softly. "I just don't know."

Dominic alternated between being a plane and a train when Sheridan joined him in the schoolyard. He stopped long enough to show her that he had his lucky coin carefully tucked in his pocket and he spoke often of his friend David. They would go to Ma's house, Dominic said happily, when David came back on the big airplane, and they'd play with the train.

After Dominic had been called into class, Sheridan stood quietly in her office for one last minute, then drove away from the Haven. Unable to face her empty house, she wandered through a shopping center until it was time to return to eat lunch with Dominic. She bought groceries in the afternoon and was at her designated post at five o'clock to kiss Dominic good-bye for the day.

Driving home, Sheridan ran her hand over the tight muscles in her neck and prayed it would not be too many hours before David telephoned. A gasp escaped from her lips as she neared her home and her eyes widened in surprise. David was leaning against the hood of a car that was parked in front of her house.

They met halfway across the lawn. They held each other, drinking in the feel and aroma of the one they had needed so terribly. Then David kissed her deeply, passionately, as tears stung the back of Sheridan's eyes.

"I missed you, Sher," he said softly.

"Oh, David, you look exhausted. Come in the house."

Inside Sheridan offered to fix David some dinner, but he waved the offer aside absently. She stared at him anxiously, seeing the fatigue, the tight set to his jaw as he paced the room in tense, jerky steps.

"What's wrong, David?" she asked finally.

"Sher, I—" He took a deep breath and sat down next to her on the sofa, grasping her hand in his two large ones. "I . . . damn."

"David?"

"Sher, Paul and I saw Uncle Vincente, and he listened to the whole story. Before we got there, he had researched every avenue open to you."

"And?"

"Babe, you're in a bad place right now. Your savings are gone and you're out of a job."

"I . . . won't be allowed to be Dominic's guardian?"

"No."

"Oh, God, David!"

"Sher, there was only one way to get Dominic out of the Haven and I did it. My mother had listed all the Cavellis as Dominic's sponsors so he could stay in this country even if something happened to her. With that kind of clout behind us Uncle Vincente obtained a temporary injunction to—to name me Dominic's legal guardian."

"What?" Sheridan whispered. "You're going—"

"I'm removing him from the school, Sher, and taking him to Los Angeles."

"Dominic?" Sheridan shrieked, jumping to her feet. "You're leaving Las Vegas with my son?"

"Listen to me," he said, standing up and gripping her by the shoulders. "I have to be in the state I have legal residence in. I have no choice but to go back to California with him. I want you to come with us, Sher."

"I can't! This is where I've established *my* legal residence for the proper length of time for the adoption proceedings. I have to stay here, in this house. My God, David, how could you do this to me? How could you take my child away from me?"

"Sher, I didn't! It's only until Paul can get to Italy and—"

"Oh, David, I'm sorry," she said, sinking onto the sofa. "I know you've done the best thing for Dominic. He must be removed from the Haven before Mrs. Alexander says things to him about me that will shatter him. I was reacting as a mother who loves her son and wants him with her. But as a psychologist, I realize this is the only solution."

"Then you'll come with us?"

In what capacity? Sheridan thought. As David's wife? Mistress? Only as Dominic's mother? What? "I'll need to know that Dominic is happy in California and is comfortable in his new surroundings. Yes, I'll go with you to help get him settled in. I need to do that, David. But then I'll have to return here to look for a job so I don't jeopardize my chances of adopting him."

"We can talk about that part later."

Dammit, David, Sheridan thought. Why didn't he make it clear right now? Did he want her to stay in Los Angeles as his wife or not? Why did he continually refuse to put that last piece in the puzzle and make it complete, whole? Why didn't he remove that shadowy doubt from her mind and allow them to start their life together? Unless he had no intention of ever doing that. . . .

"Sher?"

"What? Oh, I was just trying to sort things out. It's all happened so quickly."

"I know, babe, but it was the only way. Get packed and then we'll go pick up Dominic."

"Tonight?"

"Sher, I don't want Dominic anywhere near Mrs. Alexander. We're getting him out of there right now. I have the legal papers with me and we'll catch a plane to L.A. as soon as we get him."

"Yes, all right. I'll hurry. David, what about your father?"

"I haven't spoken with him. I told my mother about this and I suppose she'll tell him. I don't care what he thinks."

"I wish so much that you and your father would—"

"Don't worry about it. Let's get going."

Much later Sheridan leaned her head back on top of the seat, allowing the droning noise of the plane's engines to soothe her jangled nerves. At the Haven David had kept a furious Mrs. Alexander at bay while Sheridan had gathered Dominic's belongings and explained to the little boy that they were going on a big airplane with their Cavelli friend.

Dominic had clapped his hands in delight and now sat on his knees with his nose pressed to the window. The last streaks of a spectacular sunset had transformed the sky into a marshmallow wonderland of purple, orange, and yellow, and Dominic was totally enthralled.

"David?" Sheridan said. "Do you live in an apartment?"

"No, I have a house on the outskirts of L.A. It has a nice yard for Dominic to play in."

House? Sheridan thought later when they at last drove into David's driveway. Try mansion.

The ranch-style structure was enormous, and Sheridan's eyes widened as they entered the lavishly furnished living room.

"There you are," a woman said, coming out of the kitchen.

"Mom!" David said. "What are you doing here?"

"Nice welcome for your own mother. Sheridan, how nice to see you again."

"Thank you, Mrs. Cavelli."

"Call me Rosalie. Oh, hello, my Dominic Cavelli,"

she said, giving the boy a hug. "My, how much you've grown."

"I go bi pla."

"I love airplanes," Rosalie said, signing the words as she spoke. "Would you like some cookies and milk?"

"Oka. Thank you." Dominic nodded.

After she had settled Dominic at the kitchen table with his snack, Rosalie reentered the living room, where Sheridan and David were sitting together on the sofa.

"All right, Mom," David said. "What's going on?"

"Your father," she said, throwing up her hands. "I told him you were bringing Sheridan and Dominic here, and he was terribly angry to think you would have a young woman staying in your home. He raged on and on about you disgracing the Cavelli name by living in sin. So here I am as the official chaperon."

"Sweet heaven!" David roared. "I'm not taking any more of his interference! I love you, Mom, but go home."

"David, no," Sheridan said. "Please don't upset your father any further. It's me he's objecting to. He didn't want me at the Haven and he certainly can't be pleased I'm here. Don't fight him on this issue too. It will only cause more damage to your relationship."

"Big deal," David muttered.

"You're very wise, Sheridan," Rosalie said. "So! Tomorrow we're having a big picnic so Sheridan and Dominic can meet all the Cavellis."

"Oh, yeah?" David smiled. "Let me guess. The party is here and I'm paying for it."

"Of course, silly boy," Rosalie said, heading back into the kitchen.

"Wonderful," David said under his breath. "What are we supposed to do tonight? Go neck at a drive-in movie? I know my mother. She'll follow my father's orders to the letter and play warden."

"Well, there's nothing we can do about it," Sheridan said resignedly even as she ached to have David hold her and comfort her.

"Dammit, Sher, I want to make love to you."

"I know, and I—"

"Ma," Dominic said, running into the room. "My ba now?"

"Indeed you do need a bath," Sheridan said. "Off we go."

Hours later Sheridan shifted restlessly in the bed in the lovely room next to Dominic's. Rosalie Cavelli was good at her job, she thought ruefully. David hadn't been able to do more than give her a quick kiss good night when he had brought her suitcase into the room.

David's expression had been so stormy, it was comical, but now as Sheridan lay alone in the darkness the situation was far from amusing. She craved David, pictured him lying in bed just down the hall, and envisioned him taking her into his strong arms. He would kiss and caress her until she was burning with desire and then . . .

"Stop it, Sheridan," she said, punching her pillow. "You're driving yourself crazy."

At bedtime the next night Sheridan was exhausted. By midmorning David's house had been overflowing with Cavellis and she had given up trying to remember the names of the multitude of dark-haired, dark-eyed children that scurried around. No one mentioned the absence of Edward Cavelli and the remainder of the clan greeted Sheridan and Dominic with bear hugs and wide smiles.

Dominic had eyed the group warily at first, but when the older children began speaking to him in Italian accompanied by perfect sign language, his reserve vanished, and he was soon among the noisy throng. Sheridan hadn't really had a chance to see him again until she had given him a bath and tucked him into bed. She had had no private conversation with David either, and her last glimpse of him had been one of desire radiating from his dark eyes.

"Tell me about it, Cavelli," she said, flopping over onto her stomach on the bed. "This is the pits."

The next afternoon Dominic was whisked off to the zoo with one of David's sisters-in-law in her station wagon full of children. As Sheridan stood at the window to wave good-bye she felt her throat tighten as Dominic scrambled into the car without a backward glance in her direction.

That was all right, she thought firmly. Dominic was obviously adjusting beautifully and would be very happy there until Sheridan could take him home. Home to what? A quiet house with just the two of them and a train. No children to play with, no rough-and-tumble fun, no David. What if Dominic didn't want to leave Los Angeles and came to resent Sheridan for depriving him of this exciting new existence? At the picnic he had turned to Rosalie for a hug when he bumped his knee. . . .

"Oh, Dominic," Sheridan whispered. "I love you so much. Am I losing you already?"

Dominic Cavelli, she thought. He even had their name. And she was Sheridan Todd, the outsider, the only one who did not fit; for the man she loved never spoke of the marriage that would make her truly belong within his loving embrace and that of his family.

"Sher?" David said, coming up behind her.

"Hello," she said, turning to face him. "Where's your mother?"

"She went to get some groceries. Lord, Sher, I

haven't been alone with you for two seconds." He pulled her into his arms and kissed her deeply.

Sheridan melted against him, her desire soaring instantly as their tongues met and flickered against each other. David's hands slid down her back to her buttocks, urging her against his body. She felt the evidence of his arousal pressing into her as they kissed in an urgent frenzy.

"I want you, Sher," David said, close to her lips.

"And I want you, but your mother will be back and—"

"I know," he said, stepping away and raking his hand through his hair. "My father is a lousy—"

"David, don't."

"Yeah, okay. I'll change the subject. Dominic is doing great, don't you think?"

"Oh, yes. He adores the children and everyone is treating him like one of the family."

"Of course. He's a Cavelli."

"Well, yes, but David, now that I know Dominic is going to be happy here, I really must get back to Las Vegas."

"Why?"

"You know the answer to that. I've got to find a job so my adoption petition will show that I'm employed."

"Sher, we're already here, together, and Dominic is with us. What's the point in going through all those proceedings when in actuality the ultimate goal has been reached? Hey, my father is going to want his wife back. My mother will go home in a couple of days and we'll start living like normal people."

"What are you saying, David?"

"I'm asking you to stay, Sher. We love each other. I don't want you to leave and go back to Las Vegas. What would be the purpose? Everything we need is right here, including Dominic."

"You mean Sheridan Todd and David Cavelli would set up housekeeping together?"

"Together is the key word there, Sher. We don't need some silly ceremony and a piece of paper to know how much we mean to each other. Edward Cavelli may live by outdated standards, but I sure as hell don't. I want you here with me, and that's all that is important."

"Why don't you just come right out and say it, David?" Sheridan said, her voice rising. "You don't want to marry me, to make a commitment for the rest of your life. This way, when you're ready to move on to your next little adventure, there won't be all that hassle of divorcing me! You can just send me packing and be done with it."

"That's ridiculous! I love you and plan to spend the rest of my life with you. Don't you trust and believe in me enough to know that?"

"David, I don't know what to think. Your actions don't match your words. You say all those lovely things but you won't take that last step, the one that would make it legal and binding, name me as a Cavelli, your wife. You're keeping a loophole, an out, so you can cancel your part in this whenever the mood strikes."

"Dammit, Sher, that's a rotten thing to say!"

"It's true! You have nothing to lose, David, but I do. If I move here, I'll forfeit my Nevada residency and with it any hope of adopting Dominic. No, David, I won't do it. I can't. I refuse to play house with you until you get tired of the game, because then I'll have lost everything."

"You're walking out on me?" David asked, a muscle twitching in his jaw.

"I'm going home, where I belong. I'm going home to wait for my son."

"Dammit, I love you!"

"And I love you, but it isn't enough. It just isn't, David."

"I don't believe this!" he yelled. "You're basing our future, our entire life together on some damn piece of paper that will sit on a closet shelf? That's crazy! I don't need that stuff to know how much I love you. Hell, I've had enough of this. I'm going out."

"David—" she called, only to shudder as he slammed the front door behind him.

A strange numbness settled over Sheridan and, as if she were standing outside herself watching her actions, she walked into the bedroom and packed her suitcase. When Rosalie returned, Sheridan quietly explained that she was leaving shortly for Las Vegas. Rosalie's expression was one of concern and confusion, but the older woman didn't press Sheridan for an explanation.

With her last ounce of emotional strength, Sheridan lifted Dominic onto her lap when he ran in the door. With forced cheerfulness she explained that she must leave for a while, but he would have a wonderful time with David and the other Cavellis. Dominic frowned as if sorting through what Sheridan had said, and she held her breath as she waited for his reaction.

"Oka, Ma," he said finally. "I sta David hou. I love you, Ma."

"I love you, Dominic," she said, struggling against her tears as she held him tightly in her arms.

David had not returned by the time her taxi arrived to take her to the airport. After one last hug for Dominic and Rosalie, she hurried out the door, locking away in her memory the sight of Dominic's tiny face watching her from the window.

When Sheridan entered her quiet house in Las Vegas, she was exhausted. She walked slowly to the doorway of Dominic's room and stood staring at the train on the floor, hearing the mingled laughter of David and the little boy. With a shuddering breath she pulled the door closed, refusing to give in to the tears that threatened.

So now what? she thought, sinking onto the sofa. How did she rebuild her life? Where would she find the strength? David's refusal to commit himself spoke volumes. Dominic, too, held a place in David's life in the here and now with no guarantees for the future. Her only hope was that she could still eventually adopt Dominic if Paul achieved his goal in Italy. In the meantime she would have to get a job as quickly as possible. Certainly in a city of half a million people there would be a position open for a psychologist. Oh, sure, Sheridan told herself, everyone would be thrilled to hire someone who had been fired from her last position because of personal misconduct. Wonderful.

But, by heaven, she would not fold up and cry for the rest of her days. Dominic was safe for now, and she knew David would watch over him . . . at least until the novelty wore off. Paul had to accomplish the mission in Italy. He just had to! And the minute Dominic was declared a United States citizen, Sheridan would set the wheels in motion to petition for adoption. Dominic would come home!

Sheridan tore open the newspaper and carefully read the ads for employment. Nothing. Absolutely nothing in her field. She wouldn't panic. On Monday she'd register with an agency and pay the enormous fee, but she would find a job.

By six Monday night, Sheridan was exhausted. The day had been a grueling series of frustrating hours. The agency she had selected from the telephone book had been very enthusiastic when Sheridan listed her credentials. The trouble had started when the representative had contacted Mrs.

Alexander for the recommendation. The director of the Haven had viciously attacked Sheridan's morals and code of conduct, stating that Sheridan had been dismissed from the school due to inappropriate behavior. Sheridan had explained the incident at the Big Top and Edward Cavelli's outdated standards, but the representative had said that without a favorable letter from her last employer, it would be extremely difficult to obtain another job in the same field.

With a weary sigh Sheridan pushed herself off the sofa and went into the kitchen to eat a dinner she hardly tasted. Things were getting worse by the minute, and she honestly didn't know how much more she could take. She missed Dominic, wanted to hear his laughter and see his beautiful face. And in spite of the pain in her heart she ached for David, longed to be held in his strong arms. She loved him. As wrong and foolish as it was, she loved him.

The ringing of the telephone brought her from her tormented reverie, and she answered it with a subdued greeting.

"Sher?" a male voice said.

"Yes."

"This is Paul. Paul Cavelli."

"Yes?" Sheridan whispered, sinking onto the sofa.

"I'm just calling to see if you're all right. Do you need anything? If—uh—if you're short of cash, I'd be glad to—"

"Did David ask you to phone me?"

"Yeah. I'm not doing this very well, am I? He's worried sick about you, Sher. I've never seen David like this. Do me a favor and let me send you some money, okay?"

"No, Paul."

"Look, why don't you come back over here and straighten things out with David? He—"

"Paul, I can't give up my Nevada residence or this house. I still intend to adopt Dominic and I have to stay here. I can't go off for a fling in California simply because that's the mood David's in at the moment."

"He loves you, Sher."

"For now. Just like he's all enthralled with Dominic at the present time. He told me himself that he always moves forward and never looks back. David is fascinated by the way we met. He thinks it's fun and exciting, but we have no future together. I am the woman of the hour. Nothing more."

"Sher, give the guy a break. You know he had a helluva blowup with our father, and—well, everything just dumped on David at once. It really blew him away when he found out you had left L.A. Why don't you get on a plane and—"

"No! I will not do anything to jeopardize my chances of adopting Dominic. I *am* going to adopt him, Paul."

"Man, what a mess. Okay, I give up for now. I'm leaving for Italy in the morning. I'll be in touch."

"Paul, I'm so grateful to you for what you're doing in going to Italy. I don't know how to thank you."

"How about trusting my brother a little? I know how much he loves you, wants to be with you forever. I can't believe I'm reading him wrong."

"But if you are?"

"Then I'm the dumb Cavelli, I guess. I'll call you from Italy."

"All right, Paul, and thank you again."

"Hang in there. And Sher? I'd bet pasta that you haven't seen the last of David Cavelli. He's a stubborn bugger. Bye."

"Good-bye, Paul."

Sheridan slept restlessly that night and awoke

tired and edgy. At noon she called the employment agency, but the representative said she had no luck in obtaining any interviews for Sheridan and asked if she would consider accepting another line of work at least temporarily. Picturing the meager balance in her checkbook, Sheridan agreed.

That night Sheridan lifted a glass of iced tea in a silent salute to herself. She was once again among the employed. She was starting Monday morning as a clerk-typist in a doctor's office. Whoop-dee-do, she thought sarcastically. For this she had gotten her doctorate?

But it was a job and Sheridan was determined to stick it out. The pay was ridiculously low, the hours long, but it would keep her in her home and food on the table. When she adopted Dominic, she would leave Las Vegas and start fresh somewhere else. In the meantime she could put up with anything.

By the following Friday night Sheridan thought she was dying. She had never been so tired in her life. The work load at the doctor's office was beyond belief, and she had dragged herself home at the end of each day totally exhausted. Had it only been a week? It seemed like a year. She ignored the telephone when it rang, not wishing to put out the energy to say hello, but finally answered it as it continued its shrill summons.

"Sher?"

"Yes?"

"Paul."

"Yes, Paul," she said, instantly alert.

"Tell me I'm brilliant, a genius, the greatest lawyer you've ever known."

"You did it? You had Dominic declared a U.S. citizen?"

"I'm sitting here looking at the official document."

"Oh, Paul, that's wonderful!"

"I'm really something, aren't I?"

She laughed. "You sound just like David."

"Speaking of the bum, have you heard from him?"

"No, Paul, not a word. But then I really didn't expect to."

"I think he's just giving you a little space for now."

"You never give up, do you?"

"Cavellis don't quit, Sher. So, what are your plans now?"

"I'll petition to adopt Dominic."

"And what about David?"

"I have no thought beyond Dominic, Paul."

"Are you sure you're not Italian? You're awfully stubborn, Sheridan Todd."

"I can say *gelato*, but that's the extent of my Italian."

"Except maybe for the love you have for a couple of Cavellis. A certain David and Dominic? Think about it. *Arrivederci*, Sher."

"Good-bye, and thank you for everything."

Think about it. If Paul only knew the long hours Sheridan had spent through the dark, lonely nights doing just that. She would go to sleep thinking of Dominic, only to awaken a short time later yearning for David. Her body would be awash with desire, aching for David's touch, the feel of his hands and lips, his special masculine aroma. Her breasts would grow taut as she envisioned David's maddening, tantalizing journey over them. She loved David Cavelli and she always would. He had declared that she was his, and she was, would always be, even though he no longer wanted her.

Sheridan spent the weekend cleaning her neglected house and taking luxurious naps, but was still exhausted when she reported to work Monday morning. She dashed out to a telephone booth on her lunch hour to call Dominic's social worker to tell her the good news that Paul had relayed.

"Bravo," Barbara Roth said. "That is fantastic!"

"Will you file my petition for adoption, Barbara?"

"I'll get the paperwork started and turn it over to the state office as soon as I get my copy of the document from Paul Cavelli. I'll write my recommendation on your behalf too. A representative from the state will make a home visit to see Dominic's room and that sort of thing. You do understand, Sheridan, that David Cavelli, as Dominic's legal guardian, will have to approve the adoption."

"What?" she gasped.

"I suggest you contact him and see if there's going to be any problem obtaining his full cooperation."

"But he's only in that capacity temporarily."

"He's still legally responsible for the boy at this point. He'll have to agree that you are the person who should raise Dominic. The state office is familiar with you and this case. I don't anticipate any difficulties here. It's David who has the power to make or break this for you."

"I see."

"I'll talk to you soon, Sheridan."

"Yes . . . fine. Thank you, Barbara."

David, Sheridan thought, hanging up the receiver. Was that why he hadn't contacted her? Did he know he held the trump card and Sheridan would have to come crawling to him to beg for Dominic? Would he seek revenge because she had refused to stay in Los Angeles with him the way he had planned? She had no choice. She would have to call David and ask him to cooperate and say that Dominic should be with her. He would do it. Oh, God, he just had to!

The afternoon dragged by with agonizing slowness. The elderly doctor approached Sheridan at closing time, praising her for her work and saying he was delighted to have her on his staff. She thanked him absently, her mind focusing on the telephone call she would make to David that night. Somehow she would have to listen to the rich timbre of his voice without falling apart. She would try desperately not to picture his handsome face or the strong hand that would be gripping the receiver. No part of her imagination would linger on what he might be wearing or the heat and aromas she knew would be emanating from his powerful, beautiful body.

She would speak coolly, professionally. She would state her business and wait for his reply. Surely he was ready to return to his carefree bachelor life without being encumbered by a four-year-old child. He would no doubt be delighted to recommend that Sheridan receive custody of Dominic at the earliest possible moment. He might even place Dominic in her care pending her court hearing. Yes, that's what he would do! He would see a way to be relieved of the responsibility immediately!

With a renewed burst of energy Sheridan drove home and hurried into the house, snatching up David's telephone number from her desk. Her heart was racing as the first ring sounded, then she heard a clicking noise and a female voice came on the line.

"David Cavelli's answering service."

"Is it possible to speak with him?"

"No, I'm sorry Mr. Cavelli is out of town until the weekend. May I take a message?"

"He'll be away the entire week?"

"Yes. Did you wish to leave word for him to contact you?"

"No, I—I'll call again. Thank you."

Sheridan slammed the receiver into place and pressed her fingertips to her aching temples. Damn him. Where was he? And who was taking care of Dominic while David cavorted all over the place? Dominic should be in an excellent school to further his training, not dragged through heaven knew where. Or had David dumped him on his family and taken off for a good time? Damn that man! He had no concept of what it meant to be a father. But Sheridan knew what was required to be a mother and, by God, she would be Dominic's mother!

The week moved by slowly. Sheridan sat down one night and carefully scrutinized her finances. She canceled the newspaper, bought only the necessary food, and took the bus to work on days she didn't have errands to run on the way home. On Wednesday she collected her expensive prints off her wall and during her lunch break turned them over to a dealer who anticipated no difficulty in selling them. She was determined to have her bankbook in a healthier condition before it was examined by the court. Nothing, nothing would stand in the way of obtaining her goal. Not technicalities, or money, or David Cavelli.

By Friday Sheridan was again exhausted and fell into bed that night without stopping to eat dinner. She slept until noon on Saturday and immediately called David when she woke up. The syrupy voice of the answering-service woman informed Sheridan that Mr. Cavelli had been detained and was not expected back until late Wednesday night.

In a surge of frustration and anger Sheridan slammed down the receiver and then, for a lack of something better to do, instantly burst into tears.

Seven

Sheridan stared in the mirror and decided she looked terrible. She had lost weight, there were dark shadows under her eyes, and she appeared exhausted. Well, there was nothing she could do about it. David was supposedly due back in L.A. tonight and perhaps once she spoke with him, she could start sleeping properly.

When she called him at six that evening, the answering service did not come on the line. The phone simply rang and rang until she gave up and replaced the receiver. She tried again at seven and at eight, but there was still no answer. When Sheridan dialed the number at nine o'clock, she didn't really expect him to answer and nearly jumped off the sofa when she heard his gruff greeting.

"David?"

"Yes."

"This is Sheridan."

"I know your voice, Sher. What can I do for you?" he asked, his intonation cool and flat.

So that was how he was going to play it, Sheridan thought. The tough-guy routine. Okay, Cavelli, gear up—because two can dish out this pasta. "I am calling regarding Dominic."

"Oh?"

"I trust he's well?"

"Very."

"Has . . . he asked about me?"

"Of course. But you were able to make him understand that it isn't possible for you to be with him right now. He's accepted that."

"Good. As I'm sure you're aware, Paul has obtained the document I was seeking. I am now proceeding with my adoption request and I would appreciate a brief letter from you stating you are in favor of my petition."

"Why?"

"Why what?"

"Give me one good reason why I should help you."

"Dammit, David," Sheridan shouted, completely forgetting her sophisticated composure, "don't be ridiculous. You're Dominic's guardian and I need your recommendation so I can adopt him. I'm sure you're more than ready to have him out of your way."

"And what do I get out of this?"

"Get? Your freedom! I'm certain that instant fatherhood has put a cramp in your style."

"I see. That's all you're offering?"

"Lord, you're despicable! David, quit throwing your macho routine around. I'm not impressed. Why don't you just return Dominic to me immediately and be done with it?"

"Oh, I couldn't do that."

"And why not?"

"The last I heard, Sher, you were broke and out of work. How do I know you can provide a proper home for Dominic?"

"I assure you that—"

"I think I'd better come check things out for myself. I'll be over there Saturday afternoon."

"No!"

"Good-bye, Sher."

"David, wait!"

The dial tone announced that the connection had been severed and Sheridan slammed down the receiver. David was coming to Las Vegas! Oh, for Pete's sake, now what was he up to? It didn't make sense. He was making a big production out of acting like a social worker, inspecting Sheridan's home and . . . body? Ha! He wouldn't get within ten feet of her with those strong yet gentle hands and those soft, sensuous lips and— "Damn you, David Cavelli," Sheridan said, stomping into the kitchen.

How she lived until Saturday, Sheridan didn't know. She had hardly slept, could barely choke down her food, and suffered from an ongoing headache. The doctor in the office had expressed concern over her appearance and suggested she have a complete physical. Sheridan mumbled something about having sinus trouble and redirected her attention to her typewriter.

It seemed quite appropriate that Saturday was dark and gloomy; a drizzling rain fell until noon. Sheridan dressed in black slacks and a bright pink blouse, gave her house a quick dusting, and waited. She was beyond tense; she was limp. She had gone over the telephone conversation with David a thousand times in her mind, hearing his crisp tone of voice, his veiled innuendos hinting that he expected some type of payment from her in exchange for Dominic. He had sounded brutal and cold, and the remembrance sent a shiver down Sheridan's spine.

It was three o'clock sharp when she heard the car pull into the driveway. She stood and drew a deep, steadying breath, then opened the door after his sharp knock sounded.

"Hello, Sher," David said quietly.

She could only nod and step back to allow him to enter. Her heart was racing uncontrollably and a rushing noise was whirling through her head. Dressed in trim-fitting gray slacks and an open-neck royal-blue shirt, David seemed to fill the room with his presence. His familiar masculine aromas assaulted her senses and Sheridan swallowed heavily, willing her spiraling desire to stay under control. David turned and looked at her, his gaze flickering over her as a frown creased his brow.

"Have you been ill, Sher?"

"No, I'm fine. Would you care for a drink?"

"No, thank you."

"Please sit down, David," she said, waiting until he had lowered his massive frame onto the sofa and then taking the opposite end.

"I think this has gone on long enough, don't you, Sher?" David said quietly.

"What has?"

"This wide emotional circle we're dancing around each other. It's getting us nowhere. I love you, Sher, and you love me. There's really nothing complicated about it. If it's marriage you want, then—"

"It's not what *you* want, David. You've made it very clear how you feel about that type of commitment, that sense of permanence."

"I've told you more than once that you're mine. That sounds pretty permanent to me," he said, his voice rising slightly. "You were the one who walked out on me and Dominic. I asked you to stay with me, Sher."

"For how long, David? Until you got bored with the home-and-hearth bit? No, thanks. I'm staying here so I can adopt Dominic."

"You can't have him!" David roared, getting to his feet.

"What? What are you saying?" Sheridan whispered.

"I'm not giving him up! He's a part of my life now. I love that boy and I'm keeping him! If you want to be his mother, you'll have to be my wife!"

"You're crazy! Why are you doing this?"

"You leave me no choice. I can't seem to get through to you. I do love you, Sher. I admit I never placed much importance on the mechanics of a wedding ceremony. I just wanted you with me, but it's even better this way. The courts won't hesitate to grant us custody of Dominic once we're married, so—"

"Lord, this is just another business deal to you, isn't it? Your latest acquisition is a four-year-old boy, and it would go a lot smoother if there was a dutiful little wife on your arm! You said yourself you never considered marrying me. But now it will make things convenient for you, so what the hell, why not? Well, no way, David! I refuse to be a party to your deception!"

"Dammit, Sher, you're twisting everything around!"

"It's Sheridan!"

"You are *Sher*," he growled. "*My* Sher! Why are you making this so damn difficult?"

"Me? Me? You're the one who's acting like a—a tyrant. Just give me my son back and get out of my life!"

"No!"

"Dammit, David!" Sheridan jumped to her feet. "I don't understand why you are—oh." A wave of dizziness swept over her, and she reached out her hand for the sofa.

"Sher!" David shouted, and in a swift movement

scooped her into his arms and carried her into the bedroom. He laid her gently on the bed and sat down next to her. "What happened?" he asked softly.

"I don't know. The room just started spinning. I'm all right now, I'll—"

"No, don't move. Sher, you really look sick."

"Thanks a bunch!"

"I mean it. You're so thin and . . . are you working?"

"Yes."

"Where?"

"I'm a typist in a doctor's office."

"Damn. What did you do with the prints from your living room?"

"I sold them."

"Oh, Sher, why wouldn't you accept the money I wanted to send you?"

"Can you really ask that question, David?"

"No, I guess not," he said wearily.

"I'm doing fine and am perfectly capable of providing a home for my son."

"Marry me, Sher. Be my wife, Dominic's mother."

"No, David, I can't do that, not under these circumstances. Did you . . . patch things up with your father?"

"No, I haven't seen him."

"I'm sorry about that. It was all my fault."

"Let's not start that again. Sher, I'm going to kiss you. I have to before I go crazy."

"David, don't. I—"

"Oh, Sher." He moaned and placed one large hand on either side of her head, then covered her mouth in a long, powerful, searing kiss.

Sheridan was lost. Gone. All the pent-up desires burst within her in a kaleidoscope of colors as David's questing tongue found hers. Instinctively her arms reached up to circle his neck, her fingers inching into his thick hair. David's lips slid over the slender column of her neck as he deftly undid the buttons on her blouse and the front clasp of her bra. He brushed the material aside, and his lips found one throbbing breast. He drew the nipple into his mouth and Sheridan could feel it grow taut under the flickering motion of his tongue. She pulled his head closer as he directed his tantalizing attention to the other ivory mound, and she moaned softly as her passion grew.

"Let me love you, Sher. Forget everything else for now," David murmured. "Please, Sher. I want you so much."

"Yes. Oh, yes," she whispered.

It was strange how their clothes seemed just to float away, and then David was stretched out next to her. Beautiful David. Strong, wonderful David, whose kisses burned a trail over her body until she was writhing under his lambent caresses, calling his name, and aching for the fulfillment only he could bring.

Her hands roamed over his chest, to his flat stomach, to the tight flesh of his buttocks, and she felt his muscles tremble as her lips and tongue danced across his moist skin.

"Sher!" he gasped.

"Now, David. Oh, please, now!"

He slid his strong arm around her waist and pulled her up tightly against his body as he moved over her. With a thrusting, pleasure-giving force he came to her in all his magnificent glory and carried her away to the place she had yearned for so desperately. Higher they soared as the intensity grew, their bodies moving as a single entity in a perfectly synchronized rhythm. David was consuming her, filling her very mind and body and soul, and it was ecstasy. Together, as one, they reached the summit of their climb to paradise and burst upon it, each chanting the name of the other.

And then they were perfectly still, not moving, hardly breathing, each wishing to delay the return to the here and now and to the chaos of their lives. With a deep sigh David moved away then pulled Sheridan to him, his fingers twisting through the ebony cascade of her hair as he rested his lips lightly on her forehead.

"I do love you, Sher," he said so quietly, she barely heard him.

"And I love you, David, but we're worlds apart in values and—and everything. David, I will always love you. I'll be here whenever you want me. The hell with my pride. There will never be anyone else for me."

"Marry me, Sher."

"No, David. Marriage was never in your plans until all this happened with Dominic. I can't be an afterthought, a partner of convenience. When you're free to get away, you can come visit me and Dominic, and—"

"I'm not giving him up, Sher."

"Oh, David, you can't really want him. You're still trying to prove to your father how tough and independent you can be."

"There's no getting through to you, is there?" David said, sliding off the bed and reaching for his clothes.

"Where are you going?"

"Home. Home to my son."

"He's not yours!" Sheridan said, sitting up on the bed. "He's mine! Mine!"

"As the saying goes, I'll see you in court," David said, turning and striding from the room.

"David, no! Don't do this!" Sheridan screamed, but the only answer she received was the loud slamming of the front door.

She sank back against the pillows as a sob escaped her lips. He meant it! David actually intended to fight her for custody of Dominic. It was insane! Would he go to extremes of this measure to prove a point to Edward Cavelli? It was sick. Sick! David could have really thumbed his nose at Papa if Sheridan had agreed to marry the naughty son. Parade decadent Sheridan Todd under the old man's nose and see how he liked those apples!

Oh, why had she succumbed to David's touch and fallen into bed with him minutes after he walked into her living room? Because she had wanted and needed him so tremendously and was powerless to say no. Offering to become his mistress was a little much, but she wasn't sorry they had made love. It had been heavenly to be held in David's arms again, to have all that virility focused entirely on her, Sheridan thought. Sweet, sweet bliss. She loved David Cavelli and always would, but she was prepared to fight him for Dominic. The court would see that a young boy needed a mother, not a swinging bachelor father. She would win! For once in his life, David Cavelli was going to lose!

"Barbara? Sheridan Todd."

"I know you've been trying to reach me, but I was out of town."

"I saw David Cavelli, Barbara."

"Excellent. When?"

"Two weeks ago today. I've been so anxious to speak to you. That's why I called you at home on a Saturday."

"No problem. What did David say?"

"He—he plans to fight me for custody of Dominic. He wants to keep him, Barbara."

"What? Good Lord, I never anticipated he'd do anything like this."

"Barbara, what am I going to do?"

"Well, I had better contact David myself. For all we know, he's already started proceedings in the California courts. He could have adopted Dominic before your case even got on the docket here."

"Oh, no!"

"I'll get back to you, Sheridan. Give me David's phone number. He doesn't have to tell me a thing, but let's hope he'll at least inform me as to what steps he's taken."

"Barbara, if David files for adoption in California and I have Nevada residence, how can I fight him?"

"You have two separate hearings. If David's case is heard first, you could testify, showing just cause why you are the more fit parent. If you won, you'd have to turn around and convince a judge here of the same thing. David, however, would be out of the picture once he lost in the California court."

"So if I go first, he could come here and testify against me?"

"In essence, yes. He would have to prove that Dominic is better off with him. If you lost, he'd have to petition the California courts for custody."

"Barbara, I think we should stall, let David go before me. If you can find out when his court date is, I could have my say. It would have to look good in my file that I had shown the California judge that I'm a more stable person for Dominic."

"That's true, but it's risky. David could win on his first shot and the case would never get to Nevada. He could walk out of that courthouse with legal custody as Dominic's father and that would be that."

"I'm still convinced that David is playing a game with Dominic, Barbara. Let him go to the judge ahead of me. When I show up, he'll finally realize I'm not backing down. I want to go to his turf instead of him storming into mine. He'll think he has me at a disadvantage if he comes here. I'm going to be very quiet about my plans and simply appear on the day of his hearing. What you've got to do is find out when it is."

"I'll do my best, Sheridan. You do understand that you could lose Dominic that day on the coast?"

"Yes, I know."

"I'll talk to you as soon as I have any information."

"Thank you, Barbara."

It was good, very, very good, Sheridan decided as she hung up the receiver. When David heard nothing from her, he would relax and think she had given up the battle. When she showed up in court unannounced, he would be taken totally off-guard. By that time he would probably be so relieved to be out from under Dominic's care, he'd applaud her arrival. He had sounded fiercely possessive about Dominic, but it was an issue with him now, something he had to prove, points to be scored. He didn't really want a son any more than he had a burning desire to have a wife! But if David came to the Nevada hearing, he'd fight tooth and nail simply to show how much power he had. He'd drive himself to win for no other reason than Cavellis don't like to lose.

"Gotcha, Cavelli," Sheridan said. "I'm one step ahead of you this time."

Glancing at her watch, she grabbed her purse and headed out the door. She had been feeling better for the past week or so, but had experienced several more dizzy spells and had made an appointment at a free clinic for a checkup. She had been anemic on occasion in the past and wanted to be in the best physical condition possible for what was ahead.

The clinic was crowded, and Sheridan waited for over an hour before she was seen by a pleasant woman doctor who insisted on examining Sheridan from head to toe. When she was through, she instructed Sheridan to get dressed and come into the office at the end of the hall.

"I know, take iron pills," Sheridan said with a smile as she sat down in the chair opposite the doctor's desk.

"And some vitamins I'm going to prescribe."

"Oh? Well, all right."

"Miss Todd, you are pregnant. About six weeks, I would say."

Sheridan opened her mouth, but when nothing came out, she shut it and stared at the doctor as if the woman had just grown an extra head.

"You didn't suspect?" the doctor asked gently.

"I . . . no, I . . . my God," Sheridan whispered.

"Miss—Sheridan, I can see this has come as a shock to you. I really think you should go home and give careful consideration to the alternatives available to you and not make a hasty decision."

"Alternatives?"

"You can have this baby and keep it, put it up for adoption, or choose to terminate your pregnancy."

"Give my baby away? Put him up for adoption? When I'm trying to do just the opposite?"

"Pardon me?"

"I'm sorry. I guess I'm slightly hysterical."

"Is there any chance that the father will—"

"No! No, David mustn't know about this. I'll never get Dominic if—"

"Dominic?"

"My . . . son. It's very complicated. Thank you, Doctor. I'll think about what you said."

"I'll be waiting to hear from you. You do need some vitamins if you decide to—"

"Yes, yes. I'll be in touch. Good-bye."

Sheridan hardly remembered driving home. She was just suddenly back in her living room with her hands clutched tightly in her lap as a clamor of voices screamed in her head.

Pregnant. She was carrying David Cavelli's baby. What in the name of heaven was she going to do? She couldn't hide her condition for long, and there wasn't a court in the country who would grant her custody of Dominic when they discovered she was about to become an unwed mother.

"Want to trade, David?" she said out loud. "Just like baseball cards. Give me Dominic and you can have this one when it's born. Oh, God," she sobbed. "What have I done? I've lost my Dominic forever. I'll keep this baby and cherish him, but, oh, Dominic, I love you so much. I'm sorry. I'm so sorry. I've abandoned you too."

Sheridan cried. She cried for her lost Dominic; her deep love for David, which was never meant to be; and for the child within her who would not know his father. And she cried for herself. For the pain and the loneliness and the price she was paying for having answered her own needs in the arms of David Cavelli. She cried until there were no more tears to shed, and then she stopped. With a calm new resolve she knew what she must do.

The week dragged by as Sheridan waited anxiously for Barbara Roth to call with information regarding David's plans. Finally on Friday morning, Barbara telephoned her at work and a meeting was set up at a small restaurant during Sheridan's lunch hour.

"I'm always running late," Barbara said, sliding into the booth. "I finally located David, Sheridan. Apparently he took Dominic to Disneyland. Anyway, he was very cooperative and charming."

"He's been known to be extremely charming," Sheridan said softly.

"David has a court date in California in a month."

"I see."

"Sheridan, what's wrong?"

"Barbara, it won't be necessary for you to go any further in my behalf. I will not be seeking custody of Dominic."

"What? Why not? I can't believe this!"

"I'm—I'm pregnant with David's baby."

"Sheridan!"

"Ironic, isn't it? He has my son and I have his."

"Does he know?"

"No, and he never will."

"But, Sheridan, it's his child too. He has a right to—"

"No! David is liable to demand visitation rights. Barbara, he might even try to gain custody of this child too. Men with his power and money have been known to win those cases."

"Yes, you have a point there. I've handled more than one like that. But what about Dominic?"

"I don't stand a chance. No judge will give me Dominic when it becomes known I'm pregnant. I'll never see him again."

"Oh, Sheridan, I'm so very sorry. I wish there were something I could do."

"Thank you for getting this information for me."

"But why do you need it if . . . ?"

"I have one more thing to do for Dominic, Barbara. One more."

The real estate agent whom Sheridan contacted to sell her house was thrilled when he inspected the home, which was situated in a lovely neighborhood. The property was sold within a week, and Sheridan began the tedious job of packing her personal belongings. She quit her job at the doctor's office, deciding she could no longer push herself so hard and wanting nothing to happen to the baby she was carrying. She sold most of her furniture, keeping only her bedroom set and a chair, a lamp, and a table for the living room.

The first changes were coming over her body and her breasts became fuller, sensitive to her touch. A lovely glow seemed to radiate from her blue eyes and her ebony hair glistened from the constant brushing she gave it. She gained back the weight she had lost and began to detect a slight thickening of her waistline.

She had heard nothing from David and felt perhaps he was waiting her out, hovering in the background to see what her next step would be. He was aware from Barbara's call that Sheridan knew of his court date, but he didn't contact Sheridan to discuss her intentions.

Three days before David was to appear before the California judge, Sheridan paid farewell visits to Barbara and Janet and several other friends. She placed the last of her furniture along with the boxes of her personal items in storage and flew to Los Angeles, where she checked into a motel.

On the morning of the hearing she was amazingly calm. She dressed in an attractive rose-colored linen suit and twisted her hair into a chignon at the nape of her neck. At the courthouse she had to weave her way through crowds of bustling people in her search for the designated room.

And then she saw him. David. Her heart beat a sharp tattoo beneath her breast and she stopped, drinking in the sight of him. He was in a perfectly cut dark suit, his hands pushed casually into his pockets as he stood in the corridor chatting with a man Sheridan assumed was his attorney. She could feel the strength emanating from David's body as she saw the straight line of his back, the width of his shoulders. His thick dark hair was combed neatly over his ears and fell just to the collar of his shirt. Sheridan saw many women glance in David's direction, obviously appreciating his virile attractiveness.

Sheridan moved forward slowly, a determined tilt to her chin. As if sensing her presence, David turned and looked at her, their eyes meeting as the lawyer glanced curiously in her direction. David walked to her and took her hand, his gaze never leaving her face.

"Sher," was all he said.

"Hello, David."

"Oh, Sher, it's so good to see you. You look wonderful. I was worried about you since I saw you last."

"I'm very well."

"Obviously. You're beautiful. Sher, why have you come?"

"I intend to testify at this hearing, David."

"Sher, look—"

"As Dominic's psychologist, not as his mother."

"Sher, wait!" David said, but Sheridan pushed past him and entered the room, sinking onto a wooden bench as her trembling legs refused to hold her. She couldn't fall apart now. She had to do what she had come for. It was her last gift to Dominic, her parting gesture of love.

"Doctor Todd?"

"Yes?"

"I'm Michael James, David's attorney in this matter. He informs me you wish to speak here today."

"Yes, I do."

"Would you tell me what you intend to say?"

"No."

"All right, Doctor Todd." Michael sighed. "I'll ask the judge to put you on the stand."

"Thank you, Mr. James. I assumed Paul Cavelli would be representing David."

"Paul is still in Italy. Doctor Todd, David sincerely loves Dominic. I know you don't believe that, but it's true. He considers Dominic his son."

"So did I," Sheridan said softly.

"I—"

"This court is now in session," a voice said. "All rise."

Sheridan watched as David strode past her and took a chair at a table in the front of the room. After they were told to be seated, Michael James stepped forward and spoke to the judge, who glanced up at Sheridan and nodded. When Michael was seated next to David, the judge rapped his gavel and cleared his throat.

"Doctor Sheridan Todd," the elderly man said gruffly.

Sheridan took the seat next to the bench after being sworn in.

"Doctor Todd," the judge said, "it is my understanding that you have some pertinent information regarding Mr. Cavelli's petition for adoption."

"Yes, I do."

"You may proceed."

"Your honor, I was Dominic's psychologist for over eighteen months while he was a resident student at the Haven school in Nevada. I was there when Mr. Cavelli first met Dominic. It was David—uh—Mr. Cavelli who broke through Dominic's emotional fears, thereby allowing the child to function as a normal little boy."

"I see. Go on."

"There may be some question in your mind as to Mr. Cavelli's ability to provide a loving home for Dominic because Mr. Cavelli does not have a wife, a mother for Dominic. Mr. Cavelli comes from a large, close-knit family that will provide Dominic with an abundance of people who will help care for him and shower him with affection. Mr. Cavelli is also in a financial position to see that Dominic has the finest training available to further his progress in overcoming his hearing problem to the best possible level."

"So what is your professional opinion, Doctor Todd?"

"From a clinical standpoint and also as one who came to love Dominic with my whole heart, I urge you, sir, to grant David Cavelli custody of him, to make David Dominic's legal father . . . forever."

"Sher!" David shouted, jumping to his feet.

"Mr. Cavelli, I will ask you to remain seated," the judge said firmly.

"But—"

"Mr. Cavelli!"

David slumped back into his chair, his eyes riveted on Sheridan as she stepped down and walked from the room. She stared directly ahead and willed her legs not to fail her until she was out in the hall.

"Sher, please! Wait!" David called.

"Mr. Cavelli, do you wish to proceed with this hearing?" the judge asked.

"Yes. Yes, of course, I do."

"Then there will be no further outbursts in my courtroom."

"Oh, Sher," David whispered. "Oh, my Sher."

Sheridan hid behind a column in the corridor, blinking back the tears that burned at the back of her eyes. She had done it. She had made every effort possible to see to it that Dominic would have everything he would ever need. Should David tire of raising the little boy, he would be swept into the warm, loving embrace of the Cavelli clan. Dominic would have the finest schooling, the best clothes and toys, and would no doubt travel and see the world. He would have it all—except Sheridan as a mother.

The time crept by slowly, then suddenly the doors

burst open and David strode out of the room and disappeared from view. Sheridan had been unable to see his face clearly and she hurried forward as Michael James emerged.

"Mr. James, did—did David—"

"He has been named Dominic's legal father," Michael said quietly.

"Oh, thank God."

"Your statement had a great deal to do with the judge's decision. Doctor Todd, David is most anxious to speak with you. Apparently there has been a grave misunderstanding between the two of you. Please, Doctor Todd, contact David immediately."

"No, that won't be possible. I'm leaving town. I only came to Los Angeles to assure the future of Dominic."

"You won't reconsider and talk to David?"

"No."

"Is there anything you wish me to say to David?"

"Tell him . . . my name is Sheridan. There is no one called Sher anymore."

"I don't—"

"He'll understand, Mr. James. Good-bye."

Michael James watched as the beautiful young woman walked quickly down the corridor until she was swallowed up by the crowd. With a deep frown on his face and a shake of his head, he moved slowly out of the courthouse.

Eight

"I'll see you next week, Christine," Sheridan said, her hands moving in perfect sign language.

"Bye, Doctor Todd," the teenager said, dashing from the room.

Sheridan smiled and then pushed herself slowly to her feet. Her hand rested on her protruding stomach as she walked across the hall and into her living room. She switched on the lights, bringing a small Christmas tree instantly aglow. A heavy snow was falling outside, turning Denver into a marshmallow fairyland.

Christmas, she thought. In a few days it would be there, and two weeks later her baby would be born. Her baby. Not David Cavelli's. Hers.

Moving to Denver shortly after the court hearing in Los Angeles, Sheridan had purchased a small house with the money she had received from the sale of her Las Vegas home. After converting one of the bedrooms into an office, she had slowly built a clientele of hearing-impaired children who were having difficulties adjusting to their handicap. Sheridan's reputation had spread, and she now had a waiting list of families seeking her services.

She had hoped that the memories of David and Dominic would diminish in time, but they had not. She could still hear Dominic's laughter as clearly as if he were in the same room, and David's face haunted her dreams through the night. Oh, how she loved them, her son and the father of her unborn child. She could only pray that the new baby would fill the void, ease her loneliness and the ache in her heart.

Sheridan sank onto the sofa as the telephone rang, and she answered it cheerfully.

"Sher? Paul Cavelli."

Lord, no, she thought wildly. It wasn't possible. How had they found her? "Paul?" she whispered.

"I was beginning to think you'd disappeared off the face of the earth. It's taken a squad of private detectives this long to find you."

"Why were you looking for me, Paul?" Sheridan said, trying to keep her voice steady.

"David has been searching for you since the day you left the courtroom over here. There's been so many false leads, I decided to follow this one up myself so he wouldn't be needlessly hurt if it was a dead end."

"What does David want with me, Paul?"

"He desperately needs to talk to you."

"Why? Has something happened to Dominic?" she asked anxiously.

"No, the boy is fine. But, Sher, there's so much you don't understand. Listen to David. Give him a chance to explain. My father—"

"What does Edward Cavelli have to do with this?"

"He was the one who didn't rest until he had located the finest detectives in the country to try and find you. He blames himself for what happened.

Everything. He wants to see David happy again. We all do. Talk to David, Sher, please."

"No," Sheridan said, placing her hand protectively on her stomach. "Don't tell him where I am, Paul, because I swear I'll get a restraining order to keep him away from me. He got Dominic. What more does the man want from me? I have a new life now, and it doesn't include David Cavelli. I'm warning you, Paul. Keep my whereabouts to yourself, or David is going to find himself in a great deal of trouble."

"Sher—"

"Good-bye, Paul. There is nothing more to say on the subject." She hung up.

Sheridan pressed her hands to her burning cheeks and tried to think past the panic she was registering. She'd run. She'd pack her suitcase and disappear into the night. No, she couldn't. The baby was due and she had nowhere to go where she wouldn't be eventually found. The Cavellis had all the power and money needed to track her down wherever she went. Why was David doing this? He had Dominic; he had made amends with his father; his life was in order. Why was he hounding her? He couldn't come to Denver! He'd discover her pregnancy and might decide to stake a claim on his child. Having heard her threats, Paul would surely convince David to give up his quest. David would listen to Paul and leave her alone. He had to. Dear Lord, he just had to!

The day after Christmas, Sheridan began to relax. Paul apparently had gotten through to David that she meant business and would go to any extreme necessary to keep David away from her. She had spent Christmas with the family of one of her young clients and had managed to have a reasonably good time, in spite of the thoughts of Dominic and David that were hovering close to the front of her mind.

How had they spent the holiday? Sheridan wondered. Had the entire Cavelli clan gathered for a joyous celebration? Oh, what a glorious time Dominic would have had with the laughing children and the multitude of brightly wrapped gifts. Had David smiled down on his son like a proud father? Had there been a woman at David's side?

"Who cares?" Sheridan said aloud as she washed her breakfast dishes. "David can sleep with the whole Fifth Army if he feels the urge. It makes no difference to me."

Dressed in black slacks and a pleated pink maternity top, Sheridan settled onto the sofa to write thank-you notes for the Christmas gifts she had received in the mail from family and friends. She would handle emergency-only appointments from now until she was back on her feet after the baby was born, and she felt deliciously lazy and contented. The human cargo beneath her pink top gave her a hefty kick, and she patted her stomach and laughed, telling the baby to be patient for another week or so.

A knock on the door brought a frown to her face. Surely no one would have a psychological crisis the day after Christmas, Sheridan thought. But then again, she supposed they could, and pushed herself rather ungracefully to her feet.

When she opened the door, it was as though she were frozen in place, hardly able to breathe.

"Hello, Sher," David said. "I— My God, you're pregnant!"

Sheridan attempted to slam the door shut, but David pushed it back effortlessly and stepped into the house. He looked enormous, and the stormy, menacing glare on his face sent a wave of apprehension through Sheridan.

"Get out of my home," she said, annoyed at how shaky her voice sounded.

"Damn you, Sher. You're having my baby and you didn't have the decency to tell me?" David roared, shrugging out of his sheepskin jacket to reveal a black turtleneck sweater. Sheridan had the irrational thought that he looked like a threatening pirate.

"Decency!" she shrieked. "You don't know the meaning of the word. And besides, what makes you believe this is your baby?"

"I know damn well it is! That child is mine!"

"No! It's mine! You won't touch this baby, David."

"Now I understand why you showed up in court that day and helped me. You knew you'd never be granted custody when they found out—"

"That's right! And if you lost, Dominic would spend his life in an institution or being shuffled from one foster home to the next. I wanted desperately for him to have a family, a—"

"Father?"

"Yes! At least for as long as you wanted him. I knew your family would come to love him and would step in when you became bored with your new role. I accomplished my goal and I started my life over. You have no right to come barging in here like a hoodlum!"

"Hoodlum?" David said, a smile creeping onto the corners of his mouth. "Like an Italian hit man or something?"

"Shut up and get out!"

"Do you think it's a boy or a girl?"

"What?"

"Don't women have a sixth sense about these things?"

"It's a girl. David! Leave my living room!"

"And go where? The kitchen? Bedroom?"

"I'm calling the police."

"Fine. I'll tell them my dear little pregnant wife

just hasn't been herself lately. Something to do with hormones during pregnancy, Officer."

"You wouldn't."

"Oh, but I would," he said, plunking himself onto the sofa. "You know, you're beautiful when you're fat. I'm glad I didn't miss seeing you like this. When are we having our baby?"

"*We* are not having anything except a duel to the death! Go home to Dominic, where you belong."

"Can't. My mother and sister packed up the troops and took them to Florida this morning. Doesn't make much sense. I mean, it's just as warm in California as it is down there. Sure is cold here though. Is our baby warm enough?"

"David, I can't handle this. I want you out of here."

"You're forgetting something, Sher."

"It's Sheridan."

"So Michael told me. As I was saying, you've forgotten an important fact."

"Which is?"

"Since the night I caught you at the Big Top in Las Vegas, you have been mine. Still are. Always will be."

"Ha!"

"Shouldn't you get off your feet?"

"My feet are none of your business," Sheridan said, lowering herself to the sofa.

"Shall I get you a glass of milk?"

"David!"

"No, huh?"

"No!"

"I tell you, Sher," David said, locking his hands behind his head and stretching his long legs out in front of him, "you sure led me a merry chase."

"Paul has a big mouth."

"If you would have listened to me, none of this would have been necessary."

"You don't say," she snapped.

"I was desperate, Sher. When you said you wouldn't marry me, I didn't know what to do, so I decided to put a little pressure on you and adopt Dominic myself. You were supposed to complete the nice family unit, but you blew it."

"*I* blew it?"

"Sure. You handed Dominic to me on a silver platter and disappeared. You're not a fair player, Sher. You screwed up the whole thing. I love Dominic and you would have realized that if you hadn't split."

"Sue me."

"No, I'll just love you until the day I die. Man, Dominic is going to be so tickled when he has his very own baby sister. He'll go nuts."

"You can't have this baby, David."

"Of course not, sweet dope, you're the one who's pregnant, not me. We will, however, take her back to L.A. together. As man and wife."

"The hell we will."

"Don't swear in front of our child, Sher. They can hear stuff in there. I read it in a book once. Your hair is gorgeous. I've missed running my hands through it. In fact, I've wanted every inch of you, Sher-eye-dan. A man needs his woman in his bed at night, close, warm, there when he reaches for her. There hasn't been anyone since you. I'm probably eligible for the priesthood. A frustrated Italian can be a mean dude to deal with."

"You don't scare me, David."

"I don't intend to. Sure you shouldn't be drinking a glass of milk?"

"Go away."

"Nope."

"Well, I will then," Sheridan said, getting to her

feet after three attempts. "I'm going to the grocery store."

"Okay," David said, leaping up and grabbing his jacket. "I'll drive."

"Have a nice time. Good-bye."

"Where's your coat? Actually it would be better if I went for you and you stayed here and rested."

"I am going to the store!"

"And I am driving the car."

"Then will you leave?"

"We'll discuss it."

"All right." She sighed and threw up her hands. "I'll get my coat."

She had to be crazy, Sheridan decided much later as she stood in her kitchen with David at her elbow putting groceries away. Somewhere between the aisles of canned soup and detergent she had agreed to fix steak and French fries for lunch when they returned to the house. She had actually laughed right out loud when David had loaded the cart with seven gallons of milk and she refused to budge until he put most of it back. He had told the checkout clerk that Sheridan was going to have a baby girl and had purchased a book entitled *1001 Names for Your Baby*.

He had smiled at her warmly, tenderly, and Sheridan had melted under his gaze. Oh, it was good to see him, smell his special aroma, hear his nonstop chatter and deep, rich laughter. He was the most beautiful human being she had ever seen, and her heart ached with love for him. But enough was enough. They'd have lunch, and then she would throw him out on his tail!

"Tell you what, Sher," David said. "I'll cook and you go sit down."

"You?"

"Hey, I'm great. I'm not about to drag Dominic out to a restaurant every night. I've become very proficient in the kitchen. I'm not too shabby in another room either, if you'll recall."

"Priesthood, my big toe," Sheridan said, walking out of the room. "Be my guest. Cook your little heart out."

The meal was delicious and Sheridan begrudgingly said so.

"I know. I'm terrific."

"Well, it was nice of you to drop by, David. Goodbye."

"I'm not leaving, Sher," he said, looking at her steadily. "I am very much in love with you; you are about to give birth to my child; and I'm staying."

"David, what do you want from me?" Sheridan whispered.

"Your love, forever. Your last name changed to Cavelli. To hear your laughter mingling with our children's in our home. I want you, Sher, for the rest of my life."

"How can I know that? There's always extenuating circumstances. You never considered marrying me until Dominic came on the scene. Now you're probably filled with guilt over this baby. No, David. My answer is no."

"We'll see."

"I'm going to go take a nap. Please be gone by the time I wake up."

"Sleep well."

"Stuff it."

David's throaty chuckle followed Sheridan into the bedroom, and she slammed the door behind her. The man was infuriating. It was a rerun! He was all hyped up on marrying her simply because there was once again a child involved. Well, thanks, but no thanks. She was not a pathetic little creature who needed a strong man to take care of her. Oh, Lord, yes, she did. No, absolutely not! David Cavelli was going to haul his gorgeous carcass out of there and leave her alone!

When Sheridan awoke an hour later, she ran a brush through her tangled hair, then opened the bedroom door a crack and peered out with one eye. She moaned silently as she saw David stretched out on the sofa, his nose buried in the book with the 1001 baby names.

"Okay, Cavelli," she said, marching, as well as her stomach allowed her to march, into the room, "up and out."

"How about Cathy Cavelli?" David said, still looking at the book. "Or Carmelita?"

"Ugh."

"Cassandra? Oh, here we go. Clarissa Cavelli. It has a nice ring to it."

"I'm naming her Emily, after my grandmother," Sheridan said, walking into the kitchen and returning with a glass of milk. She waved at David to make room for her on the sofa.

"Oh," David said, swinging around and sitting up. "Emily Cavelli. It's not too bad."

"Emily Todd," Sheridan said as she sat down.

"Wrong. Good girl, drink every bit of that. I washed the dishes. Did you sleep?"

"Yes. David, you're upsetting me. It's not advisable for someone in my condition."

"You're right. I won't say another word."

He folded his arms over his chest and began to hum terribly off-key while Sheridan clenched her teeth. She lasted approximately three minutes before she exploded.

"Stop it!" she shrieked. "You're driving me up the wall!"

"Gosh, Sher, I was just sitting here minding my own—"

"You're giving me the crazies. Ow!"

"What's wrong?"

"Nothing. Emily just kicked me."

"Where?" David asked, leaning over and peering at Sheridan's stomach.

"There she goes again. Here." She picked up David's hand and rested it on the protruding area. "Can you feel that?"

"My God," David whispered. "I've never in my life . . . Sher, that's our baby! Doesn't that hurt? She's really dancing a jig in there. Are you in pain? Oh, Sher, I can hardly wait to see her, hold her in my arms. My daughter. And Dominic is my son and you are mine. I'm the luckiest man in the world. Tell her to knock it off now, Sher. She's beat you up enough for one day."

"Oh, David." Sheridan laughed. "You're so funny sometimes. Okay, Emily, did you hear your father? Go to sleep."

"You said it, Sher," David said, turning her face toward him by gently cupping her chin in his hand. "You called me her father, and I am. I'll love her just as I do you and our son. Marry me, Sher. It's time to come home."

David slowly moved forward and covered Sheridan's lips with his. It was so sweet, so soft, and a sob caught in Sheridan's throat. She lifted her arms to circle his neck, drawing him nearer, savoring his taste and sensuality. Oh, it was heaven. She was with David, where she belonged, held safely in his strong arms. David would take care of her. They'd be a family. Sheridan, David, Dominic, and Emily Cavelli. The Cavellis. The group. The gang. The whole outfit.

"I don't think Emily would approve of what I have in mind here," David said, taking a ragged breath and sitting straight up. "I should go jog."

"It's snowing."

"I'll build a snowman. Sher, don't you see how

happy we're going to be? And Dominic will stop having his nightmares and—"

"What nightmares?" Sheridan said, an instant frown on her face.

"I discussed it with the psychologist at his school. He said Dominic has been through a lot of changes lately and had adjusted very well. But whenever I have to go out of town he stays with my sister, or mother, or one of my brothers. It's the nights that get him because he's not always in his own bed. But once you're there—"

"You can just go on your merry way and have a great time," Sheridan said, her voice rising. "Wouldn't it be easier to hire a live-in housekeeper than be saddled with a wife?"

"For Pete's sake, Sher . . ."

"You're incredible, David! Every time I start to believe in you and what you're saying, the truth manages to rear its head. You've got it all figured out, haven't you? Set old Sher up in a big fancy house and solve the problem of what to do with that nuisance of a kid when you want to go off on one of your flings."

"Dammit, you're twisting things around again. Why do you always have to do that? What are you going to do? Get all in a huff and disappear again? No way, Doctor Todd. That's a Cavelli baby you're carrying, and you're not taking off with my child!"

"I'll do what I damn well please!"

"Don't push me, Sher. Don't threaten me with any hint that you might try to keep that baby from me," David said, his face stormy as a muscle twitched in his jaw. "You seem determined to think the worst of me. My telling you how much I love you means nothing to you. But don't get any ideas about trying to separate me from Emily."

"Or what?" Sheridan yelled. "You'll flex your

money-and-power muscles and take her away from me just like you did Dominic?"

"Just when was it you stopped loving me, Sher? Did it hit you all at once or come in stages, a little at a time?" He shrugged into his jacket. "I'm going for a walk, but I'll be back. Don't try to lock me out or I'll kick the door down. I'm sticking like glue because you're not pulling a disappearing act on me. I'm staying close to *my* daughter. Have you got that, Sher? My daughter!"

The door was slammed with such force that a picture on the wall rattled precariously and then settled at a tilted angle. Sheridan sat perfectly still, her eyes wide as she drew a shuddering breath.

When had she ceased to love David Cavelli? she asked herself. Never. She loved him with an intensity that was beyond definition. But she didn't know what to believe! He moved so fast, made statements that contradicted what she prayed was true, and left her in a sea of turmoil and confusion.

But she had seen it. A haunting pain had crossed David's face, radiating from the fathomless depths of his eyes as he had said she no longer loved him. As angry as he had been, the vulnerability had been there, a look of desolation and helplessness. He had searched for her for months and then pushed aside his own needs and spent Christmas with Dominic before coming to Denver. He had explained that the steps he'd taken in petitioning for custody of Dominic had been a desperate attempt to convince her that he sincerely loved the little boy and wanted Sheridan as his wife.

Sheridan had questioned his remark regarding her role as a convenient baby-sitter while he cavorted around the country. But had his statement actually been wrong? He was envisioning his son safely tucked in his own bed, his wife caring for their children until he could return. He worked extremely hard for the Cavelli empire, threw himself into his job with the same intensity with which he loved.

With which he loved. Oh, yes, he did love her! He didn't weigh his words before he spoke, he simply stated his thoughts honestly as they came to his mind. Nothing phony or rehearsed, just a man expressing his feelings, and she had stood in judgment of everything he said, dissecting it and examining it for the slightest flaw.

And the baby she was carrying? He had accepted Emily as a wonderful gift, an extension to his existence. Again his reaction had been quick and real. His child was about to be born and he was thrilled beyond belief, already picturing Dominic holding his baby sister. He saw them all as a family and had expressed his love for Sheridan time and time again.

"Oh, David," she whispered, "what have I done to you? I've been so wrong, so hateful. You're right, David. It's time for me to go home. With you. Forever."

Was it too late? Had she crushed David's love and belief in her? Could she convince him that she truly did love him and wanted, needed, to be by his side as his wife, the mother of his children? When he returned from his walk in the snow, would he allow her to pull him to her and beg his forgiveness? Had she damaged his Cavelli pride once too often? What consequences would she pay for her thoughtless, hateful words?

Sheridan pushed herself off the sofa and walked to the window, praying she would see David emerging from the thickly falling snow. There was no sign of his massive frame, but she would wait. Wait just as he had during the long months he had searched for her.

For the next hour Sheridan moved restlessly through the house, returning often to the window, only to resume her pacing. Suddenly a gripping pain shot through the lower regions of her body and she gasped, stumbling to the sofa and easing herself carefully to a sitting position. She told herself firmly to relax, that she had merely gotten tense and had spent too much time on her feet. When the tearing agony ripped through her again a few minutes later she pressed her hands on her stomach and held herself rigid.

"No, Emily," she said, a sob catching in her throat. "Not yet. Your father isn't here. Please, baby, we need David."

Sheridan looked at the clock, and when another pain came eight minutes later, and six minutes after that, she knew she had to act. She telephoned her doctor, who agreed to meet her at the hospital, then called for a taxi. She placed the remaining items in her already packed suitcase, stopping once as a spasm seized her.

"Oh, God," she whispered. "I'm so frightened."

Just as she re-entered the living room, David burst in the door, more angry than Sheridan had ever seen him. "I sent your damn taxi away!" he roared. "You were really going to do it, weren't you? I warned you, Sher."

"David, no! I had to call for a ride. The baby is coming."

"What?"

"Oh!" Sheridan gasped, and clutched her stomach.

"My God, Sher," David said, hurrying to her side. "Did you phone the doctor?"

"Yes, he . . . said to go to the . . . hospital. I . . ."

"Put your coat on. Let's get out of here."

The roads were slick with ice and the visibility poor, so David had to drive with agonizing slowness. He pulled over to the side of the road several times and got out to clear the snow from the windshield since the wipers couldn't move the heavy, wet load. Sheridan clenched her teeth and silently waited for each wave of hot, gripping pain to tear through her body. David did not speak after asking directions to the hospital. His knuckles were turning white under the pressure he was exerting on the steering wheel, and his jaw was set in a tight hard line.

At last the hospital came into view and David drove into the emergency area, shutting off the ignition and taking off for the entrance at a run. He reappeared moments later with a nurse and an orderly, who was pushing a wheelchair. Sheridan was helped from the car and before she could even turn to look for David was whisked into the building and down a corridor.

The next hours were a blur. Sheridan seemed to move in and out of a foggy world that was made up of pain and people speaking in hushed tones. She called for David, begged someone, anyone, to bring him to her side, only to be told she must relax and not become upset. Then she apparently had done something right as she was lifted away from the tormenting bed and taken to a room that glared with bright lights.

She had to do as she was told so the agony would end and she could escape. She pushed and panted and gripped an unfamiliar hand and . . . Emily was born! With an indignant wail the tiny creature made her presence known as she pulled up her arms and waved tiny fists in the air.

"She's beautiful," Sheridan said, tears pouring onto her cheeks.

"Look at that headful of hair," a nurse said. "She's just adorable."

"She's half Italian," Sheridan said as Emily was placed on her stomach.

"And has the temper to prove it." The doctor chuckled. "You can play with her later, Mother. It's nap time for you."

When Sheridan opened her eyes, she blinked several times in an attempt to clear the cobwebs from her mind. As the reality of where she was struck her, her hands flew to her flat stomach. A lovely smile lit up her face as she remembered her Emily. Emily Cavelli, the daughter of Sheridan and David.

A slight movement in the room caused Sheridan to turn her head. David was standing by the window, staring out, his hands shoved deeply into his pockets.

"David?" she said.

"Hello, Sher," he said, walking over to the edge of the bed. "How are you feeling?"

"No worse for wear. Have you seen Emily?"

"Yes, she looks exactly like me. I guess Italian genes are pretty heavy-duty."

"She's beautiful, like her father," Sheridan said, acutely aware that David had not yet smiled.

"The father she was never supposed to know," he said, a bitter edge to his voice.

"I was wrong, David. I've made so many mistakes. Can't we put everything behind us and start over? I want to marry you and—"

"Oh, really? That's a quick changeover." He raked his hand through his hair. "Why now? Or did you realize I was serious about having my daughter near me?"

"I love you, David."

"You're playing games, Sher. You don't believe even half of what I say. You can't love a man you don't trust. I'm tired of beating my head against a brick wall where you're concerned. I'll marry you, but on my terms."

"What do you mean?"

"We'll live in the same house and I'll give you anything you want. You'll be a mother to Dominic and Emily and present the picture of the perfect wife to the whole Cavelli clan. I'll ask nothing of you except that. You'll be free to leave whenever you choose, but if you do, it will be alone. The children will be mine."

"We can't survive like that, David! It wouldn't be a marriage, it would be a sham!"

"Make a decision. Come back to L.A. with me as my wife or be prepared to lose Emily in a court of law."

"My God, David!"

"Well?"

"You leave me no choice. I'll have to go with you. I thought . . . you loved me."

"And I believed you loved me. Can't win them all. I'll make the arrangements and be back later." He turned and walked from the room.

"Oh, David," she said, covering her face with her hands. "I waited too long to tell you how much I love and need you. I've been such a fool."

Sheridan was enveloped in a deep, crushing depression that had swept over her like a heavy shroud. It wasn't until Emily was brought into the room and placed in her arms that Sheridan registered a glimmer of hope. Emily was a miniature David, with her thick crop of black hair, tawny complexion, and huge dark eyes. Even her fingers were long and tapered like David's and her eyelashes an identical fringe around her eyes.

David would love his beautiful daughter as he already loved Dominic, and Sheridan would be there. She would not give up until she and David had reclaimed what they once had. Through her own harsh accusations she had driven David away, but, God willing, he would come to forgive her, believe in her again. Sheridan would hold out her arms to welcome him and pray he would move into her embrace. David had constructed a protective wall around his heart, and she would tear it down brick by brick, if it took her the rest of her life.

Nine

"Ma," Dominic yelled, running into the room, "Emily wake up."

Sheridan laughed. "Did you tickle her again?"

"No, Ma. Emily hungra."

"All right. You climb up on the sofa and I'll let you give her the bottle."

"Oh, boy!" Dominic said, dashing from the room.

In a few minutes Sheridan was sitting next to Dominic as Emily lay on a pillow placed across her big brother's lap. Dominic held the bottle with both hands and concentrated on his task. At six weeks, Emily was a happy, thriving baby who smiled at the slightest provocation.

Six weeks, and in that length of time David had not touched or even kissed Sheridan. He was devoted to the children, appeared relaxed and carefree around the other Cavellis, but barely spoke to his wife. When the house was quiet for the night, David would retreat to his den or leave altogether with no explanation as to where he was going.

Sheridan's resolve to win back David's love was slipping fast. She had told him two days before that the doctor had cleared her to resume sexual activity, and David had simply nodded and continued to read the newspaper. Again that night they had lain far apart in the big bed in their room. After David had fallen asleep, Sheridan had crept into the living room and cried until she was exhausted. She couldn't reach him. David looked at her as though she were a stranger, someone he had never really known. The only time she saw him smile was when he was with Emily or Dominic. The pleasant expression he plastered on his face when they were in the company of the other Cavellis never reached his eyes, although his family seemed oblivious to any problems between the newlyweds.

"Drink good, Emily," Dominic said, and Sheridan smiled down at her two beautiful dark-haired children.

The reunion with Dominic had been a moment Sheridan would cherish forever. David had carried Emily into the enormous home while Sheridan stepped cautiously into the living room. Dominic was sitting on the sofa being shown a picture book by Rosalie Cavelli and had not heard them enter. When Rosalie touched Dominic's arm and pointed at Sheridan, he had looked up in shock. No one moved for several long minutes and then Dominic had shouted, "Ma!" and run into her arms. She had hugged him until he demanded his release. He had then lifted his small hand and brushed the tears from her cheeks.

"You sta my hou, Ma?" he had asked, a frown crossing his face.

"Oh, yes, Dominic. I'll stay forever."

Sheridan had had such high hopes after the quick wedding ceremony in Colorado and the flight to Los Angeles with her husband and new daughter. David had taken care of everything, selling her house and informing her patients that she was leaving the area. He had brought her home as he had said he wished to do, then had ignored her ever since.

"Daddy!" Dominic yelled, causing Emily to jerk in surprise.

"Hey, Champ," David said with a wide smile as he strode into the room. "What are you doing there?"

"Feed Emily. Eat, Emily. Right now!"

"Maybe she needs to burp," David said, lifting the baby to his shoulder and patting her gently on the back.

"You're home early, David," Sheridan said.

"There's a petting zoo set up in the shopping mall. I thought I'd take Dominic over."

"I'm sure he'll enjoy that. I could put Emily in the stroller and come with you."

"It's too crowded and dusty. I don't think she should go."

"All right, David." Sheridan sighed. "Have a good time."

Emily fell asleep shortly after David left with Dominic and Sheridan wandered restlessly through the house. She couldn't go on like this, but she had no choice. Nothing would tear her away from her beloved children. But, oh, Lord, how she ached for David. She loved him so much, needed and wanted to be held in his protective arms, to make love that would carry them away to their private place. Desire stirred within her when he walked into the room, when he emerged from a shower with a towel draped low on his hips, when he inadvertently touched her as he slept.

The sweet, wonderful children filled a section of Sheridan, satisfied her nurturing instincts. But the woman in her was empty, lonely, longing desperately for the man she loved. How would she survive the years ahead, living in the same house with David without his love? The children would grow, need her less and less, and she would have nothing.

With a weary sigh Sheridan walked into the kitchen and began to prepare dinner. The mealtime conversation would focus on the trip to the petting zoo. When Dominic and Emily were put to bed, the evening would stretch out into endless hours of solitude.

"Ma, I saw a lamp," Dominic yelled as he ran into the kitchen an hour later.

"A what?"

"Lamb," David corrected with a laugh as he followed Dominic.

"Oh, how nice." Sheridan smiled. "If you two gentlemen will wash up, I'll put dinner on the table."

"Come on, Champ," David said. "Let's scrub."

"I tell Emily about the lamp."

"Don't you tickle your sister, Dominic Cavelli," Sheridan said. "She's sound asleep."

The dinner conversation, as Sheridan had predicted, was a lengthy dissertation on the animals at the zoo. While Sheridan cleaned up, David played a game with Dominic. Emily gurgled in her infant seat. Baths were given, an abundance of kisses exchanged, and the children were asleep for the night. Sheridan picked up her needlepoint and wandered into the living room, surprised to see David standing by the small bar.

"Would you like a sherry?" he asked.

"Yes, thank you. That sounds very nice."

They settled themselves on opposite ends of the sofa. Sheridan watched David out of the corner of her eye as he stared into his glass.

"Are you happy here, Sher?" he asked softly.

"To a degree. Emily and Dominic bring me a tremendous amount of joy, but it's . . . not enough."

"I know."

"What happened to us, David? We loved each other so much."

"I never stopped loving you, Sher. I just started protecting myself. You never believed what I said; you found fault with every move I made. I never tried to take Dominic away from you. I thought I was doing the best thing for him—for us. Sher, every night when I turn onto our street, I wonder if you'll be gone. I can't go on like this."

"I'll never leave you and the children, David."

"How do I know that?"

"I once believed you would grow tired of being a father. I was terribly wrong. I don't know how to convince you that I love you and want to truly be your wife. I do love you, David."

"It haunts me, Sher, to think you would have never told me about Emily. Every time I hold her, I realize how close I came to not knowing my own daughter."

"I was frightened, David. I had lost my son and you. That baby was all I had. Oh, David, why can't we put the past behind us? You were the one that said you always moved forward. Can't we do that? Together?"

"I don't know," he said, getting to his feet and placing his glass on the bar. "I really don't."

"David," Sheridan said, walking to where he stood, "trust me. I love you with my whole heart."

With a moan David pulled her into his arms and claimed her mouth in a searing kiss. Sheridan leaned against him as she returned his ardor, their lips moving frantically against each other's. David's hands slid over the soft slope of her buttocks, pulling her up against him as Sheridan sank her hands into his thick hair. Tears spilled over onto her cheeks as she molded herself to the hard contours of his body. She could feel his arousal and rejoiced in the knowledge that he wanted her as she did him.

Suddenly David stiffened and pulled away. "No, Sher," he said, shaking his head. "Until I can believe you are my wife forever, I won't make love to you. It's as though there's a black cloud hanging over my head. I never know from one day to the next if you'll pack up and run off. I nearly went crazy all those months I was looking for you. I can't go through that again. If we make love, I'll be lost. I'm keeping you at arm's length to guard against what you might do."

"David, what more do I have to prove? I'm here, raising your children, telling you I love you more than life. What else, David? Tell me what I should do to convince you I want to be your wife, that there's nowhere else on this earth I want to be."

"I want to believe you! I want us to have it all. But, dammit, Sher, I've got to be sure and I'm not!" He took a deep breath. "I'm going out."

"David, don't leave. We need to talk."

"There's nothing more to say. I need time. Time, Sher." He quickly strode out of the room.

A small smile began at the corners of Sheridan's lips and grew to a bigger one. David loved her! He truly did. He was hurt and wary, but he loved her, and that knowledge would give her the strength to go on. She would never leave him. Never. And he would come to realize that.

Sheridan saw little of David for the next week. He was out of town for three days and hid out every evening in his den when he returned. They played with the children together, attended Rosalie Cavelli's birthday party, and said very few words to each other in private. Sheridan counted each day as one more in her favor. She was there, she was smiling, and she would wait Mr. Stubborn Cavelli out.

David was becoming so irritable, it was almost comical. He slammed around the house when he couldn't find his car keys—which turned up in his pocket. He threw the tantrum of the year when the newspaper boy sailed the evening edition onto the roof, and roared like a wounded bear when he tripped over Dominic's plastic truck. Sheridan simply smiled serenely and went about her appointed rounds.

"Where in the hell is my gray tie?" David said one morning as Sheridan tugged on her jeans.

"Next to the gray and black one."

"No, it is not! Oh. Yes, it is."

"You're welcome, David."

"Thank you!"

"Emily is ten weeks old today, David."

"So hire a brass band."

"Just thought I'd tell you."

"I know how old my daughter is, Sher."

"Of course, you do, dear," she said sweetly.

"What's with you, Sher?"

"Me?"

"Forget it. I'm going to work."

"Have a nice day . . . darling," Sheridan sang out.

She . . . had . . . had it! David Cavelli was going to be up for the Crab of the Year Award at this rate, and Sheridan was finally fed up. It was time to take matters into her own hands.

"Your give-me-time number is done, Cavelli," she said, marching from the room. "You are dead meat!"

She waited impatiently until she knew Paul was in his office and then called him, informing his secretary it was an emergency.

"What's wrong?" Paul yelled.

"Nothing. Want to take me to lunch?"

"For lunch you scare me to death?" Paul said something in Italian that Sheridan decided sounded like one of those nifty phrases she'd prefer not to be translated.

"My treat?" she said hopefully.

"Okay, cuckoo lady, Mama Luigi's at one."

"Thank you, Paul. Ta-ta."

The next call was to Rosalie Cavelli, who immediately said she would be happy to baby-sit that afternoon.

"Great," Sheridan said. "Uh, Rosalie, do you think you could watch the kids for a few days while David and I go out of town?"

"Praise the Lord. You're going to do something about that boy."

"Pardon me?"

"I am not a stupid woman, Sheridan. I know things are troubled between you and David. This is very good. *Buono, buono.* You take him away and make sweet love with no babies to worry about except maybe the one you are starting together."

"I didn't realize you knew that we were— Well, so be it. But, Rosalie, David and I aren't exactly going on a honeymoon. In fact, he has no idea I'll even be around at first."

"What marvelous plot do you have, Sheridan? Tell your Rosalie everything."

Sheridan filled her mother-in-law in on the diabolical plan, and Rosalie whooped in delight.

"Oh, what I wouldn't give to be there," Rosalie said. "It's so terrible, it's wonderful. Bless you, Sheridan. I know now how much you love my son."

"I do love him, Rosalie. So very, very much."

"He's so bullheaded that David, just like his father."

"But they're gorgeous."

"Ah, yes. All Cavellis are beautiful, including you, Sheridan. I am so thrilled with your idea to win back my son."

Paul, however, was not quite so enthusiastic.

"Are you crazy?" he said to Sheridan over lunch. "David will kill me when he finds out I got him there on false pretenses. Think of my wife! My starving children!"

"Are you quite finished? When can you leave?"

"Tomorrow," Paul said miserably. "Why postpone the inevitable? Do you think my wife will remarry after I'm murdered?"

"Probably."

"You're a cold person, Sher."

"And you're a doll."

"Well, David has been hell to get along with lately. Let's hope this fixes him up."

"I'm praying," Sheridan said softly.

Later that night, Sheridan pulled David's suitcase out of the closet.

"I'll help you pack," she said cheerfully.

"You seem awfully pleased that I'm leaving town," he said gruffly.

"Don't be silly. You know we'll miss you."

"Yeah. Man, Paul could have given me a little warning. He's all fired up over this land he wants me to see outside of Las Vegas."

"I'm sure he knows what he's doing."

"I'll be staying at the MGM if you need me, Sher. Damn, he's got us booked on such an early flight, I'll be up before dawn."

"Tsk, tsk."

Sheridan stood in the doorway the next morning and waggled her fingers at David as he drove away. When he was safely out of sight, she ran back to the bedroom and pulled her suitcase out of the closet. Once packed, she prepared breakfast for a sleepy Dominic and carefully explained that Grandma Cavelli would be taking care of him and Emily while she went on a big airplane like Daddy.

"Oka." He nodded. "Grandma give me pri."

"She gives you too many surprises, young man," Sheridan said with a laugh. "Oh, do not tickle your sister while I'm gone."

When Janet picked up Sheridan at McCarran Airport in Las Vegas, the vivacious blonde was even more talkative than usual.

"Sheridan, it's so good to see you. I really am so excited you're here. And to be included in on this nutsy idea of yours is more fun than I can remember. Lord, I hope it works. I know how much you love David. He's acting like such a nerd."

"Is everything arranged for tonight?"

"Yep."

"Thanks a million."

"My pleasure. I can hardly wait!"

At eight o'clock that night Sheridan was in the dressing room at the Big Top as Janet tugged on the zipper of the skimpy pink satin costume.

"It's even smaller than the first time," Sheridan said, frowning.

"Did you grow?"

"My breasts are fuller since I had Emily. Lord, this is obscene!"

"I love it. Head for the ladder, Sheridan. I'm going out front so I don't miss anything. Are you sure Paul will be able to get David over here?"

"He promised to tie him up and drag him if he had to. Oh, Janet, I'm getting nervous."

"Tough up. It'll be great."

The outfit was too tight for Sheridan to take a deep breath as she shuffled out of the room in the sloppy slippers. She mumbled a greeting to Barney, who followed her up the ladder. Once seated on the swing, Sheridan decided to forget the whole stupid plan, but before she could announce that fact, Barney released the hinge and she went swooping out over the crowd, her long ebony hair billowing out behind her like a cloud.

What was it about trapeze swings that made her have to go to the bathroom the minute she got on them? Sheridan thought dismally as she scanned the throng of people below her for David and Paul.

For the next fifteen minutes Sheridan examined the top of every head that paraded under her creaking perch. Suddenly she saw them! Paul was pulling David by the arm in the direction of the blackjack table where David had stood on the stool to rescue her. She caught a glimpse of David's stormy expression and grimaced before he turned into a wide set of shoulders directly below the midpoint of her travels.

Hardly breathing, Sheridan swung back and forth several times trying to get a visual line on her target, mentally willing David not to move. She wiggled her feet out of the pink slippers and held them precariously on the ends of her toes. Then as she passed over David, she dropped them!

Bull's-eye! They landed smack-dab on the top of his head!

David jumped in startled surprise and grabbed at the foreign objects as his head jerked up. When he saw Sheridan, his mouth dropped open. He stared at her for several long moments as she smiled brightly at him, wiggling all her fingers and toes in greeting.

As if coming out of a trance he bellowed, "Sher, what in the hell are you doing up there?"

It was amazing. It really was. How such a big, noisy place could become so deathly quiet so quickly was simply amazing!

"Hi, David," Sheridan called cheerfully.

"Sheridan Cavelli, you get down off that damn thing!"

"Nope."

"Why not, for Pete's sake?" he roared as Paul edged away from him.

"Because, David Cavelli, I asked you to start our relationship over and you refused, so I'm doing it for us. We met the night I was on this swing and you said you'd keep me forever. Well, you bum, you're throwing me right out the window and that makes me mad!"

"Sher, come down here!"

"No! I love you, David. I have never stopped loving you."

"Hey, buddy," a man yelled, "I'll take her if you don't want her!"

"Shut up!" David bellowed. "Sher, you know I love you!"

"You'd better tell her again, man," a male voice interjected.

"You love me?" Sheridan said. "Ha! Then why don't you trust and believe in me?"

"Yeah," a big burly man said. "How come?"

"Sher, I do! I just boxed myself into a corner. I was so afraid I had waited too long and you wouldn't forgive me for the way I've been acting."

"Do you forgive him, Sher?" a woman called. "Oh, do, honey. He's the most gorgeous man I've ever seen."

"Do you really love me, David?"

"Oh, God, yes. Sher, you are my life. I'm so sorry, babe. I've messed things up so badly. I love you, Sher-eye-dan Todd Cavelli, and I will forever!"

A thundering round of applause and a deafening cheer went up from the crowd. Paul collapsed against the table and let out a sigh of relief. Sheridan nodded to Barney, who grabbed the swing as she came within his reach, and she carefully climbed down the ladder. When she was several rungs from the bottom, David snatched her off, spun her around, and pulled her close to his chest as her feet dangled in the air.

"You are the craziest, most wonderful woman in the world," he said, a broad grin on his face.

"You caught me. Gonna keep me?"

"Oh, you bet I am. You are mine. Forever."

She smiled. "How nice."

"I love you, Sher. Please, please forgive me for doubting you."

"I do, David. None of what has happened matters. We're starting all over."

David lowered his head and claimed her mouth in a passionate kiss that was interrupted by someone shouting, "Go for it, man!" David scowled and set Sheridan on her feet, his eyes raking over her figure in the satin costume.

"Good Lord," he said, taking off his sport coat and sticking her arms into the sleeves.

"You liked it the first time I wore it."

"But now you're my wife."

"Am I?" she asked softly. "Am I truly your wife?"

"You're about to find out just how much I mean it."

"Heavens, what happened to Paul?"

"He's probably hiding, afraid I'll deck him for being your partner in crime."

"Your mother knew all about it too," Sheridan said smugly.

"You ganged up on me and I am so glad you did. I've been such an idiot, Sher."

"You're right."

"Thanks a lot!"

"My feet are freezing."

"Let's get out of here. Now I understand why Paul insisted we get separate rooms at the MGM. He was going on about coming down with a cold, and he'd better not breathe into my air space or something. He was hoping I'd be having the need for privacy tonight. And, my sweet Sher, I do. You and I are going to close the door on the world. I've got a lot of time to make up for."

"Lead on, Cavelli!"

David announced that he wanted to carry Sheridan into the dressing room for old time's sake, but she said that was not a red-hot idea and scampered in to change her clothes. Janet hugged her tightly and said the whole thing had been the most romantic scenario she had ever seen, while Candi hollered to David to "Come on in, darlin'!"

Outside the Big Top, in the glow of flashing lights from the casinos, David pulled Sheridan into his arms and kissed her, oblivious to the various reactions they received from those that passed them.

"You're in my arms, Sher," he said when he finally lifted his head. Desire was evident in his ebony eyes as he gazed at her. "Welcome home, my love."

"This is where I belong, David," she whispered.

At the MGM David locked the door behind them and held out his arms to his wife. Sheridan's heart was soaring with love as she nestled against him. They came together with a newfound intensity, each kiss, each tender touch, erasing the hurt and confusion of the past. They rediscovered the mysteries of each other, staked possessive claim to what was theirs to have, and soared at last to their private place above the stars.

At the Big Top Paul bought a round of drinks for a group of people he didn't know and raised his glass in salute to the trapeze swing overhead. The city of Las Vegas twinkled under the desert sky, beckoning all to come and partake in its excitement and multitude of offerings.

Inside the quiet room high above the ground, Sheridan and David were oblivious to everything except each other. David kissed away Sheridan's tears of happiness and declared his love time and time again. Sheridan held him in her arms, smiling and contented, knowing at long last that they would share all their tomorrows.

EDITOR'S CORNER

Don't be surprised when you see our LOVESWEPT romances next month. No April Fool's joke . . . but we do hope to make you smile when you see our books on the racks. We've had a makeover! Our cover design has been revamped for our upcoming second year anniversary of the publication of LOVESWEPT. Ours is a svelte and lovely new look that doesn't just keep up with the times, but charges ahead of them. And the new colors are exquisite. We believe our new image is sophisticated and modern and we hope you enjoy it. Do let us know what you think.

We've other anniversary surprises in store for you . . . but not the least of them is some delightful romantic reading!

Warm and witty Billie Green leads off next month's LOVESWEPT list with her unforgettable love story, **DREAMS OF JOE,** LOVESWEPT #87. Imagine a famous hunk of a professional quarterback coming to live in a small town to coach the high school football team. Then add a beautiful young widow with two children . . . and a town full of the most warmhearted matchmakers. Now you have the delightful premise of **DREAMS OF JOE.** And for a long time, poor Abby thinks all she *will* be able to do with Joe is dream about him . . . because all those well-meaning folks who are throwing them at one another are also forever on hand! Oh, utter frustration! Oh, the resourcefulness needed to get a little privacy for some ordinary courtin'. We're sure you'll love every minute of Billie's high-spirited love story and that it will inspire a few dreams of your own.

Showing remarkable versatility, Joan Bramsch, noted

for her humor, has given us a heart-wrenchingly beautiful and sensual love story in **AT NIGHTFALL**, LOVESWEPT #88. Hero Matthew is a man with a handicap that is new to him, frightening, and cuts him off from all he loves best to do in the world. Then suddenly heroine Billy Theodore, a warm and honest woman, intrudes into his life . . . and lights it up! She adds a sense of fun and play to his existence while he frees her to know a new and delicious sensual awareness. But for both of them there seems a time on the horizon when they must part—especially when a miracle occurs! **AT NIGHTFALL** is a truly memorable romance.

We're very pleased to introduce you to the work of Anne and Ed Kolaczyk, a long and happily married couple, whose writing you've enjoyed in other romance lines and mainstream novels as well. But before they've always published under pen names. You'll read all about how they came to write together in their biographical sketch next month, but now let me hurry to a description of their charming debut book for us. **CAPTAIN WONDER**, LOVESWEPT #89, features a hero who *is* a hero! Mike Taylor is an actor who has achieved vast fame as television's Captain Wonder. Fleeing a mob of fans, he is befriended by heroine Sara Delaney's twin daughters. Those little girls are just as wild for the muscular marvel as others, even insisting their mom wear a Captain Wonder nightshirt, yet they are soothed in his presence. Not so Mom! Mike has a most unsettling effect on her. And, as circumstances draw them together on a trek that ends at Mike's California home, they find their attraction to one another irresistible! But, there's a key question: can an ordinary smalltown woman face up to a life in the fast lane with a famous television star? The answer is heartwarming in this love story you won't want to miss!

Joan Elliott Pickart is becoming a regular on the LOVESWEPT list, as well as a real favorite! No where is her talent in creating riveting romances more evident than in her offering next month, **LOOK FOR THE SEA GULLS**, LOVESWEPT #90. Record temperatures prevail when Tracey Tate arrives in Texas to write a story on Matt Ramsey's Rocking R ranch. Immediately, too, the temperature soars within his air-conditioned house as these two fiery personalities clash . . . and learn to love. But like his father, Matt cherishes his land which he has always put ahead of everything else in life. And Tracey finds herself to be a very possessive woman where her heart is concerned. How these two sensual, emotional people resolve their conflicts makes for the very best in romance reading!

We hope you'll agree with those of us who work on the LOVESWEPT line that we've provided you with four equally wonderful romances next month. And of course we're sure you won't miss any of them—even with that high-fashion new look on our covers!

Sincerely,

Carolyn Nichols

Carolyn Nichols
  Editor
LOVESWEPT
Bantam Books, Inc.
666 Fifth Avenue
New York, NY 10103

Dear Loveswept Readers,

On the pages that follow you will find an excerpt from my new Bantam novel, PROMISES & LIES. Publication of this is an exciting event for me, and I thought I'd share with you a little of the story and how I came to write it.

I think the development of a person is fascinating, like taking a blank canvas and watching design and color create form. I wanted to do this with a young woman, and Valerie Cardell, the heroine of PROMISES & LIES, became this young woman. Three men at different stages of her life influence and help shape the woman she becomes because I believe that without romance and love, no woman's development is ever complete! I also have long been fascinated by sibling rivalry, especially between sisters, and in PROMISES & LIES, Valerie's road to happiness is often made rocky and treacherous as a result of her sister.

I set out to write a modern-day Cinderella story because I still believe in fairy tales, especially one with love, romance, danger—and of course, a happy ending. Like you and me, the heroine of this novel has her fantasies, and the fun of writing the story was that I could make sure all her dreams came true!

Happy Reading!

Susanne Jaffe

Susanne Jaffe

They drove in silence, Valerie pretending to herself that she did not know what was about to happen. He was taking her to his apartment and he was going to make love to her. That's what she wanted too, wasn't it? He would kiss her, whisper encouraging love words to her, and touch her and touch her and touch her until her skin was on fire. He would find out she was a virgin. She had to tell him. Would that turn him off? No, he would be proud that she was giving him such a special gift. And he would be gentle with her. But he might also be disappointed and she could not bear the thought of that.

Valerie had gone out with Teddy for more than three months, and had considered getting married, but had not been able to have sex with him. She had known Roger Monash for less than two weeks and she was worrying about not being able to please him in bed. She never questioned her feelings for him or what the outcome of this intimacy would be. Irrational, illogical, uncharacteristically impetuous as it might be, Valerie knew she loved him. She could not conceive of his feeling differently. The very intensity of her emotion bespoke its rightness. She did not think she was being naïve, only truer to herself than she had ever been before. And she was too innocent and inexperienced to understand the vast difference between longing and loving. She had no qualms, therefore, about doing the right thing, only about doing it right.

"Is this where you live?" she asked tremulously as they climbed the stairs of a small apartment building near downtown Dallas.

"Uh, no, this belongs to a friend of mine."

"Why can't we go to your place?"

"I loaned it out to a buddy. I wasn't sure you and I would be using it, and besides, he's married, so if I can help the poor sucker out, why not?"

Valerie nodded her understanding, but her stomach gave a funny little lurch.

"Roger, maybe we should wait," she said when they entered the apartment. It was a dismal place, with a hodgepodge of dusty furniture and a view of a parking lot. "I'm sure your place is much nicer and—"

"Who gives a shit about nice. All I care about is that I want you." He crushed her against him and kissed her deeply. "Now tell me," he whispered against her ear, "do you really want to wait?"

She shook her head and smiled up at him, eyes glistening with love. "Roger," she said softly, stepping slightly out of the circle of his arms. "I'm a virgin."

His laugh was a crude, harsh snort that Valerie pretended not to hear. "Sure. And I'm Santa Claus. Come on, get serious. If there was ever a stew who was a virgin she'd be kicked out for poor job performance."

"It's true," she said, ignoring the quick stab of hurt.

He looked hard at her. "You're telling me the truth, aren't you?" She nodded. "Why me?"

She tilted her head, surprise evident on her face. "Because I love you."

Roger Monash did not answer immediately, but a frown flashed across his Kennedy-like face, as if he was considering just how much of a bastard he really was. What he saw as he looked at Valerie was a lovely young face filled with trust, and a body that had been tormenting his dreams for a week. She had to lose it sometime, he thought selfishly, it might as well be to him.

"I love you too, baby," he said as he took her back in his arms. "And I won't hurt you. I promise."

"Could I have a drink?"

"Sure."

She followed him into a sliver of kitchen and watched him fumble around looking for the liquor and glasses. Without asking what she wanted, he poured her a glass of Scotch, neat, and she gulped it down, grateful for its warmth. She was beginning to feel chilled, as if only now the cold reality of the situation was dawning on her.

Then she was being led into a bedroom, and Roger was kissing her, his tongue prying her lips apart, his hands roaming over her back, to her shoulders, down to her hips. "Val, oh, Val, you feel so good, baby," he murmured against her ear. His hands were on the cool skin of her back as he pushed up her sweater; then he was unhooking her bra, lifting it away. He lowered his head, and his tongue caressed first one nipple, then the other, his breath scorching her as much as his touch.

"Take off your clothes. I can't stand this another minute."

"Roger, maybe—"

"I said get undressed." He turned away and took off his clothes, unaware that Valerie had not moved. She tried to unbutton her skirt, but her fingers were trembling so badly that she could not grip the button. Her sweater and bra were still bunched up over her breasts, her hands dangling by her sides. She felt miserable, foolish, incapable of doing anything to help herself.

When Roger was naked, he faced her. Whatever embarrassment and awkwardness she might have experienced during her first encounter with a naked man was mitigated by her awe at his physical beauty. His muscles rippled like those of a thoroughbred stallion. Shoulders, chest, tapering waist; lean, firm thighs: this was a body of power, a body almost audacious in its perfection. Her eyes followed the mat of sandy hair on his chest to its thinning trail, then darted up again to meet the grin on his face.

"Come on, honey, don't be shy," he said softly. "I'll help you."

Seconds later she was naked, on her back, willing herself to feel the warmth that Roger's kisses and touch usually inspired in her. But she felt oddly dispassionate as he murmured in her ear, kissed her neck and breasts and nipples and stomach, touched her in secret places and sacred places. Was it fear that had taken control, or was it something deeper, more vital? Thoughts suddenly fled as she felt him throbbing against her thigh, and then he hoisted himself above her.

"It'll hurt for a second and then it'll be fine," he assured her, and she kept her eyes wide open, nodded, wishing it was over, wishing more that she would feel something, even the pain.

* * *

It was from three this morning until five that Valerie had permitted herself to dwell on what she had done. Until then, she had found things to occupy her thoughts, to keep her from remembering how pleasureless Saturday night had been, and how a repetition of the sex Sunday afternoon and evening had left her similarly unmoved. She told herself that it was her fault; she was inexperienced and therefore scared, inhibited, inept, inadequate. She still loved Roger, she told herself; he had been kind and thoughtful each time. If it bothered her that Sunday they had gone straight to his friend's apartment and had stayed there all day, she let herself be convinced that Roger's needs were more urgent than her own, and that once the newness became part of a practiced routine, they would do things together, things that had nothing to do with sex. She told herself that he would never grow bored with her as he had with Wanda Eberle. She told herself that she had not been used.

In those two hours when night was at its

unfriendliest and morning seemed a light at the end of an infinite tunnel, when time turned threatening and thoughts turned to unavoidable truths, Valerie was thankful that Linda was sleeping. Whatever she was telling herself, she knew she would not be able to say it to Linda with any conviction. But now, as they walked together silently to get their uniforms, she had a feeling that the confrontation was imminent.

"Should I start or will you?" Linda asked quietly, keeping her eyes straight ahead.

"I suppose it will have to be you because I have nothing to say." Valerie despised herself for acting this way. She did not resent her friend's prying because she knew it came from caring. She was scared of Linda—scared to hear her speak with knowledge that Valerie would refute without sincerity.

Linda stopped and reached out to hold Valerie back from walking ahead. The two girls faced each other, Valerie's expression challenging and proud. Linda's eyes shone with anger.

"You went to bed with him, didn't you?"

"Who?"

"Who! How many could there be?"

"If you mean Roger, the answer is yes."

Linda shook her head in amazement. "Didn't I warn you? Didn't I tell you what he did to Wanda? How could you be so stupid, Val? How?"

"If you think it's stupid for two people in love to do what comes naturally, that's your problem, and I'm sincerely sorry for you," she said haughtily.

"In love! You're an even bigger fool than I thought," Linda yelled.

"I don't have to listen to this!" Valerie started to walk away, but Linda's hand was on her arm.

"Do you really think he's in love with you? Be honest, do you?"

"He said so and I believe him."

" 'He said so and I believe him.' You're incredible, you really are."

"I would appreciate your not repeating everything I say. And I suggest that we save this little chat for another time. We're going to be late."

"We have plenty of time, and besides, this won't wait. You've been deliberately avoiding me since Saturday and I—"

"I haven't noticed you trying to be with me, either," Valerie cut in.

"Of course not, you idiot. What did you want me to do, rush up and ask for a blow-by-blow description! I figured that you would *want* to talk with me—that what happened to you was important and you would want to share it with a friend. Obviously, you're so ashamed you can't even face me. That's why I knew I had to bring it up first."

"I am *not* ashamed!" Valerie retorted hotly. "What Roger and I did was beautiful and special. We're in love with each other. Why won't you believe me?"

Linda took a deep breath, briefly shut her eyes, and said: "I do believe you, Val. I believe that you love him and that you think he loves you. But let me just ask a few questions, okay?"

Valerie nodded, dreading what was coming.

"Did he take you to a friend's apartment, saying his was too far or that he had loaned it to a married friend? Did he tell you that he couldn't fly for wanting you so badly? Did he take you to bed Sunday and stay there with you all day? Did he say he can't make plans for when he'll see you next, it depends on his schedule? Did he—"

"Stop it, stop it!" Valerie shrieked, covering her ears with her hands. Gently, Linda lowered them and took Valerie in her arms. Soundlessly, Valerie sobbed, for being a fool and a coward.

"I'm sorry," Linda said softly. "I didn't want to have to hurt you this way, but I didn't know what else to do. You had to see what was going on, what kind of bastard you were getting involved with."

"How did you know he said those things to me? How did you know about his friend's apartment?"

"The answer to the first question is easy. He used the same lines on both me and Wanda. As for the second, while you've been out of it these past few days, I asked around a little. It seems that Mr. Swinging Singles Monash shares an apartment with three other guys, two to a bedroom. When he's in Dallas, he hits on anyone he knows who has a place to himself."

For a moment Valerie said nothing, staring at her roommate but seeing beyond her to the dingy, dreary, unkempt apartment with its parking-lot view. "What am I going to do?" she whispered.

"What do you want to do?"

"I *don't* want to go to bed with him again."

"Not good, huh?"

"Well, I'm sure it's my fault, but no, not too good."

"Why do you think it was your fault?"

"I'm not very experienced, after all, so I probably don't know what I'm doing."

"Your pleasure comes from *his* knowing what to do, kiddo, not you."

"Well, still, I think I'll save sex for another time."

"Another man, Val, not another time. Roger Monash simply was not the right man. Not for someone like you."

"Why *not* someone like me?" Valerie demanded, tired of being different, of being unable to do what other grown women did. What made her so special? What made her so unable to pretend?

"Because your innocence won't disappear no matter how many men you have, even if they're all like Roger Monash," Linda said with a small smile. "You deserve someone who can appreciate that innocence. I'm not saying he has to love you, Val, but there are men who will recognize your purity and admire it. If you want to experiment with sex, do it with them, not with selfish bastards like Monash."

Valerie thought about what Linda said. "You're not like that, are you?" she asked gently. Linda shook her head. "Why not? What makes me this way, and why am I so embarrassed by it?"

"Oh, Val, don't ask me questions like that. I'm not smart enough to answer them."

"You're smarter than I'll ever be," Valerie said miserably.

"No, just not as nice."

The girls looked at each other and broke into laughter, but for Valerie the sound was bittersweet. She would be seeing Roger the next night and she did not know how to tell him there would be no sex. She had a feeling that telling him she did not love him would not matter as much to him.

#1 HEAVEN'S PRICE
By Sandra Brown
Blair Simpson had enclosed herself in the fortress of her dancing, but Sean Garrett was determined to love her anyway. In his arms she came to understand the emotions behind her dancing. But could she afford the high price of love?

#2 SURRENDER
By Helen Mittermeyer
Derry had been pirated from the church by her ex-husband, from under the nose of the man she was to marry. She remembered every detail that had driven them apart— and the passion that had drawn her to him. The unresolved problems between them grew . . . but their desire swept them toward surrender.

#3 THE JOINING STONE
By Noelle Berry McCue
Anger and desire warred within her, but Tara Burns was determined not to let Damon Mallory know her feelings. When he'd walked out of their marriage, she'd been hurt.

Damon had violated a sacred trust, yet her passion for him was as breathtaking as the Grand Canyon.

#4 SILVER MIRACLES
By Fayrene Preston
Silver-haired Chase Colfax stood in the Texas moonlight, then took Trinity Ann Warrenton into his arms. Overcome by her own needs, yet determined to have him on her own terms, she struggled to keep from losing herself in his passion.

#5 MATCHING WITS
By Carla Neggers
From the moment they met, Ryan Davis tried to outmaneuver Abigail Lawrence. She'd met her match in the Back Bay businessman. And Ryan knew the Boston lawyer was more woman than any he'd ever encountered. Only if they vanquished their need to best the other could their love triumph.

#6 A LOVE FOR ALL TIME
By Dorothy Garlock
A car crash had left its marks on Casey Farrow's beauty. So what were Dan

Murdock's motives for pursuing her? Guilt? Pity? Casey had to choose. She could live with doubt and fear . . . or learn a lesson in love.

#7 A TRYST WITH MR. LINCOLN?
By Billie Green
When Jiggs O'Malley awakened in a strange hotel room, all she saw were the laughing eyes of stranger Matt Brady . . . all she heard were his teasing taunts about their "night together" . . . and all she remembered was nothing! They evaded the passions that intoxicated them until . . . there was nowhere to flee but into each other's arms.

#8 TEMPTATION'S STING
By Helen Conrad
Taylor Winfield likened Rachel Davidson to a Conus shell, contradictory and impenetrable. Rachel battled for independence, torn by her need for Taylor's embraces and her impassioned desire to be her own woman. Could they both succumb to the temptation of the tropical paradise and still be true to their hearts?

#9 DECEMBER 32nd . . . AND ALWAYS
By Marie Michael
Blaise Hamilton made her feel like the most desirable woman on earth. Pat opened herself to emotions she'd thought buried with her late husband. Together they were unbeatable as they worked to build the jet of her late husband's dreams. Time seemed to be running out and yet—would ALWAYS be long enough?

#10 HARD DRIVIN' MAN
By Nancy Carlson
Sabrina sensed Jacy in hot pursuit, as she maneuvered her truck around the racetrack, and recalled his arms clasping her to him. Was he only using her feelings so he could take over her trucking company? Their passion knew no limits as they raced full speed toward love.

#11 BELOVED INTRUDER
By Noelle Berry McCue
Shannon Douglas hated

Michael Brady from the moment he brought the breezes of life into her shadowy existence. Yet a specter of the past remained to torment her and threaten their future. Could he subdue the demons that haunted her, and carry her to true happiness?

#12 HUNTER'S PAYNE
By Joan J. Domning
P. Lee Payne strode into Karen Hunter's office demanding to know why she was stalking him. She was determined to interview the mysterious photographer. She uncovered his concealed emotions, but could the secrets their hearts confided protect their love, or would harsh daylight shatter their fragile alliance?

#13 TIGER LADY
By Joan J. Domning
Who *was* this mysterious lover she'd never seen who courted her on the office computer, and nicknamed her Tiger Lady? And could he compete with Larry Hart, who came to repair the computer

and stayed to short-circuit her emotions? How could she choose between poetry and passion—between soul and Hart?

#14 STORMY VOWS
By Iris Johansen
Independent Brenna Sloan wasn't strong enough to reach out for the love she needed, and Michael Donovan knew only how to take—until he met Brenna. Only after a misunderstanding nearly destroyed their happiness, did they surrender to their fiery passion.

#15 BRIEF DELIGHT
By Helen Mittermeyer
Darius Chadwick felt his chest tighten with desire as Cygnet Melton glided into his life. But a prelude was all they knew before Cyg fled in despair, certain she had shattered the dream they had made together. Their hearts had collided in an instant; now could they seize the joy of enduring love?

#16 A VERY RELUCTANT KNIGHT
By Billie Green
A tornado brought them together in a storm cel-

lar. But Maggie Sims and Mark Wilding were anything but perfectly matched. Maggie wanted to prove he was wrong about her. She knew they didn't belong together, but when he caressed her, she was swept up in a passion that promised a lifetime of love.

#17 TEMPEST AT SEA
By Iris Johansen
Jane Smith sneaked aboard playboy-director Jake Dominic's yacht on a dare. The muscled arms that captured her were inescapable—and suddenly Jane found herself agreeing to a month-long cruise of the Caribbean. Jane had never given much thought to love, but under Jake's tutelage she discovered its magic . . . and its torment.

#18 AUTUMN FLAMES
By Sara Orwig
Lily Dunbar had ventured too far into the wilderness of Reece Wakefield's vast Chilean ranch; now an oncoming storm thrust her into his arms . . . and he refused to let her go. Could he lure her, step by

seductive step, away from the life she had forged for herself, to find her real home in his arms?

#19 PFARR LAKE AFFAIR
By Joan J. Domning
Leslie Pfarr hadn't been back at her father's resort for an hour before she was pitched into the lake by Eric Nordstrom! The brash teenager who'd made her childhood a constant torment had grown into a handsome man. But when he began persuading her to fall in love, Leslie wondered if she was courting disaster.

#20 HEART ON A STRING
By Carla Neggers
One look at heart surgeon Paul Houghton Welling told JoAnna Radcliff he belonged in the stuffy society world she'd escaped for a cottage in Pigeon Cove. She firmly believed she'd never fit into his life, but he set out to show her she was wrong. She was the puppet master, but he knew how to keep her heart on a string.

#21 THE SEDUCTION OF JASON
By Fayrene Preston
On vacation in Martinique, Morgan Saunders found Jason Falco. When a misunderstanding drove him away, she had to win him back. She played the seductress to tempt him to return; she sent him tropical flowers to tantalize him; she wrote her love in letters twenty feet high—on a billboard that echoed the words in her heart.

#22 BREAKFAST IN BED
By Sandra Brown
For all Sloan Fairchild knew, Hollywood had moved to San Francisco when mystery writer Carter Madison stepped into her bed-and-breakfast inn. In his arms the forbidden longing that throbbed between them erupted. Sloan had to choose—between her love for him and her loyalty to a friend . . .

#23 TAKING SAVANNAH
By Becky Combs
The Mercedes was headed straight for her! Cassie hurled a rock that smashed the antique car's taillight. The price driver Jake Kilrain exacted was a passionate kiss, and he set out to woo the Southern lady, Cassie, but discovered that his efforts to conquer the lady might end in his own surrender . . .

#24 THE RELUCTANT LARK
By Iris Johansen
Her haunting voice had earned Sheena Reardon fame as Ireland's mournful dove. Yet to Rand Challon the young singer was not just a lark but a woman whom he desired with all his heart. Rand knew he could teach her to spread her wings and fly free, but would her flight take her from him or into his arms forever?

#25 LIGHTNING THAT LINGERS
By Sharon and Tom Curtis
He was the Cougar Club's star attraction, mesmerizing hundreds of women with hips that swayed in the provocative motions

of love. Jennifer Hamilton offered her heart to the kindred spirit, the tender poet in him. But Philip's worldly side was alien to her, threatening to unravel the magical threads binding them . . .

#26 ONCE IN A BLUE MOON
By Billie Green
Arlie was reckless, wild, a little naughty—but in the nicest way! Whenever she got into a scrape, Dan was always there to rescue her. But this time Arlie wanted a very *personal* bailout that only *he* could provide. Dan never could say no to her. After all, the special favor she wanted was his own secret wish—wasn't it?

#27 THE BRONZED HAWK
By Iris Johansen
Kelly would get her story even if it meant using a bit of blackmail. She'd try anything to get inventor-genius Nick O'Brien to take her along in his experimental balloon. Nick had always trusted his fate to the four winds and the seven seas . . . until a feisty lady clipped his wings by losing herself in his arms . . .

#28 LOVE, CATCH A WILD BIRD
By Anne Reisser
Daredevil and dreamer, Bree Graeme collided with Cane Taylor on her family's farm—and there was an instant intimacy between them. Bree's wild years came to a halt, for when she looked into Cane's eyes, she knew she'd found love at last. But what price freedom to dare when the man she loved could rest only as she lay safe in his arms?

#29 THE LADY AND THE UNICORN
By Iris Johansen
Janna Cannon scaled the walls of Rafe Santine's estate, determined to appeal to the man who could save her animal preserve. She bewitched his guard dogs, then cast a spell over him as well. She offered him a gift he'd never dared risk reaching for before—but could he trust his emotions enough to open himself to her love?

 # LOVESWEPT

Love Stories you'll never forget by authors you'll always remember

☐	21603	**Heaven's Price #1** Sandra Brown	$1.95
☐	21604	**Surrender #2** Helen Mittermeyer	$1.95
☐	21600	**The Joining Stone #3** Noelle Berry McCue	$1.95
☐	21601	**Silver Miracles #4** Fayrene Preston	$1.95
☐	21605	**Matching Wits #5** Carla Neggers	$1.95
☐	21606	**A Love for All Time #6** Dorothy Garlock	$1.95
☐	21609	**Hard Drivin' Man #10** Nancy Carlson	$1.95
☐	21610	**Beloved Intruder #11** Noelle Berry McCue	$1.95
☐	21611	**Hunter's Payne #12** Joan J. Domning	$1.95
☐	21618	**Tiger Lady #13** Joan Domning	$1.95
☐	21613	**Stormy Vows #14** Iris Johansen	$1.95
☐	21614	**Brief Delight #15** Helen Mittermeyer	$1.95
☐	21616	**A Very Reluctant Knight #16** Billie Green	$1.95
☐	21617	**Tempest at Sea #17** Iris Johansen	$1.95
☐	21619	**Autumn Flames #18** Sara Orwig	$1.95
☐	21620	**Pfarr Lake Affair #19** Joan Domning	$1.95
☐	21621	**Heart on a String #20** Carla Neggars	$1.95
☐	21622	**The Seduction of Jason #21** Fayrene Preston	$1.95
☐	21623	**Breakfast In Bed #22** Sandra Brown	$1.95
☐	21624	**Taking Savannah #23** Becky Combs	$1.95
☐	21625	**The Reluctant Lark #24** Iris Johansen	$1.95

Prices and availability subject to change without notice.

Buy them at your local bookstore or use this handy coupon for ordering:

Bantam Books, Inc., Dept. SW, 414 East Golf Road, Des Plaines, Ill. 60016

Please send me the books I have checked above. I am enclosing $_____ (please add $1.25 to cover postage and handling). Send check or money order—no cash or C.O.D.'s please.

Mr/Ms_____

Address _____

City/State_____ Zip_____

SW—3/85

Please allow four to six weeks for delivery. This offer expires 9/85.

LOVESWEPT

Love Stories you'll never forget by authors you'll always remember